Carolyn—
Hope you enjoy the book!

Barbara Elaine Cornelius Pasano

To my great grandmother, Inga Ohlsdotter,
whose story is in these pages.

www.mascotbooks.com

Sweden's Child

©2017 Elaine Cornell. All Rights Reserved. No part of this publication may be reproduced, stored in a retrieval system or transmitted in any form by any means electronic, mechanical, or photocopying, recording or otherwise without the permission of the author.

For more information, please contact:
Mascot Books
620 Herndon Parkway #320
Herndon, VA 20170
info@mascotbooks.com

Library of Congress Control Number: 2017909296

CPSIA Code: PBANG1017A
ISBN-13: 978-1-68401-331-9

Printed in the United States

Sweden's Child

ELAINE CORNELL

PROLOGUE

Time alone heals yesterday's wounds
And makes the past grow dimmer
Worlds forgotten, dreams of youth,
Where pain and heartache simmer
Waiting for the best of days
In ruination's glimmer
Sparking terror once again

Ida waved to the last of the guests as they left her house. She turned to look at all of the beautiful flowers in the foyer, the living room, and the parlor. Even the landing on the stairs was full of roses, chrysanthemums, ferns, and gladioli, the typical funeral flowers of Southern California, winter or summer. She turned and gently raised her hands to her white hair, lifted the black lace veil, then pulled the jeweled hatpin out of her black pillbox. Taking the small hat off and setting it on the oak hall tree, she looked into the foyer mirror and saw an ancient old woman staring back at her as she patted her hair, which had gone askew when she had taken off the hat. A feeling of deep depression came over her as she thought of her husband lying under the grass at Inglewood Cemetery, and a silent tear trailed down the creased face and slid toward her chin.

She always thought she would be the first to go considering her early childhood, her health problems, and her life experiences. She turned toward Hildur, her caretaker, who waited patiently by the kitchen door for orders.

"Well, we did it, Hildur."

"Ya, Miss Ida, Jag jus need to clean de last of de kaffe cups, de caterer haf gone vid de rest. Vy don't du lie down vid your feet up?" Hildur sang in her melodic Swedish-English, which belied the fact that she had lived in the United States for nearly twenty years.

"I will, but first I want to see something I've been meaning to look at for a long time."

Ida climbed the curved iron staircase and went down the long, wood-lined hall to her large bedroom. Walking briskly to her black silk jewelry box, she dug to the bottom to find an old skeleton key, the kind pirates used to open ancient trunks that hid jewels and gold doubloons in them. Turning back to the open door, she proceeded down the flowered carpet where a narrow door that led to the attic stairs could barely be seen in the tongue-and-groove raised paneling. Up the narrow, steep stairs she climbed and then opened the attic door, peering at the dust mites raised as the rush of air preceded her into the room. Paying no mind to the dust and cobwebs, she walked slowly, putting each foot carefully in the dusty attic. She waited for her eyes to adjust before walking around the hazy room lit only by a small dormer on each end. Spying an antique, black turtle-back trunk in the corner, she weaved between the discarded lamps, chairs, and bed frames until she stood in front of it. The size of a small blanket chest, the dusty trunk still captured the adventures of the young girl who had painted the top with a picture of the steamer that had brought her from Sweden in 1890. The picture was a copy of a penny postcard she had bought in London while waiting to embark. The large black ship sailed on a dark blue sea; there on the deck stood a tiny person with long hair blowing in the wind. Ida ran her hand across the trunk top while remembering the length of time it had taken her to paint this picture and the others on the four sides, painted when she was homesick for Bräkne-Hoby and her mother; she had lived in the attic of a Chicago mansion without friends or family at the age of sixteen. It was in the summer of the year she had run away.

She knelt beside the old trunk, letting her black silk mourning dress drag in the heavy dust. Carefully, she put the key into the old lock and, shaking with a slight palsy, turned it. The lock sprung open and her hands began to shake more as she slowly lifted the lid. Ida felt as if she were opening Pandora's Box. It contained the memories of misery and terror which drove her away from Sweden fifty-eight years before. But it also contained her family heirlooms, pieces of her homeland, and the diaries she kept as a young girl in a strange new place.

Setting the top drawer of the trunk, with its faded and stained wallpaper design, out onto the floor, she began to remove the memories of her life: a handmade sweater, a folk costume for holidays, her wedding dress, a linen tablecloth and matching napkins made by her sister, a long wall hanging made by her great-great-grandmother that they had hung at Christmastime, a favorite dress she had worn to the Columbia Exposition in 1893, newspaper articles about a mass murderer and newspaper clippings of the fair. Underneath lay the things she was looking for: a homemade dictionary of American and Swedish words, a small scrap of linen with embroidery on it for her mother, and a small black book filled with memories of days gone by.

Ida picked up her tattered black diary. Beside it lay a small box that contained a brooch of a tiny fairy holding a pale pink heart, an old envelope with a letter from her grandmother, and the remnants of money printed in Sweden. As she wiped the dust from crumbling, aged tissue paper separating the items, a rush of cold air rifted through her hair and suddenly the image of her husband, in his prime, stood before her. Ida looked at the apparition, which held out its hand and started to reach for her.

"You're dead, my love."

"I know," he softly whispered, "but I'll live as long as someone remembers me. You may not see me, but I'm here." And as she watched, the image slowly faded into the background of stacked boxes and lampshades.

She picked up the small, tattered book and started to cry before she even opened it. The tears from the day's events, and others that had taken place in years gone by, welled up in her eyes and spattered upon the book's dusty cover.

Why did she torture herself by remembering the broken English of a sixteen-year-old girl? It was time for her grandchildren to read the diary. They were living in the modern world of 1948 and had never known the ways and language of the old country. The story must be told. It must be given to the youth, so they would know the sorrow and the reason she and many others had left everything for a better life.

"Vy Miss Ida, vy er du up her in dis dusty place? And vy sit here and cry alone?"

"My grandchildren must know why I am the way I am, because in the end, when I am gone, they will know themselves better and I will live in their hearts."

"Come, let me help du to your rum," said Hildur, dismissing Ida's words as an old woman's prattle. As she helped Ida to her feet, Hildur carefully placed the old diary and box in Ida's hands and then placed the other things back into the trunk between the tissue paper and mothballs. Leading Ida through the maze of furniture, she admonished the elderly woman for coming up alone. When they reached the landing, she carefully dusted off the black silk dress and gently helped Ida to her bedroom and into the old wooden rocking chair that sat near a window.

"Du sit her, Miss Ida, while I get du some tea." And with a quick look back at her employer, she hurried through the hall and down the stairs to the kitchen. After setting the copper teapot of fresh, cold water on the stove to boil, she looked for the doctor's phone number in the address book on the table. Finding it, she hurriedly dialed his number and waited for an answer.

"Hey, Doktor Skoglund, det har Hildur, Frau Ida's huskeeper. Jag tink Misses Ida is in a bad way. Ya, vi buried Herr Bergstrom today. Vill du komma over later? Tack så mycket."

Ida opened the small, tattered book to the first page and read the faded words like they were written yesterday. In her mind, they had been. The mirror showed a white-haired lady dressed in black silk, looking very prim and proper, but she felt sixteen, wild and free.

1891 June 13

I dag go I till Chicago. It is city jag no från Fru Anderson, who teach me English ven I er smal. Min sister Hanna vill hav en yob for me. Soon will be min första dag as American. I vill tala English so no man nos jag komma från Sweden. I vill hav nu nam so no man från Sweden vill no me. I vill go till skola and I vill get rich and go till Sweden to get min mor...

Sitting in her mother's old chair, Ida closed her eyes and rocked. She didn't have to read the diary to remember the story. Her thoughts went back to another time and another country, where her dreams were so vivid. Little did she realize then that her innocent dreams would foretell the future.

CHAPTER 1
May 1889

Come one and all to the pasture
Come one and all to the sea
The flowers now bloom
Small birds sing their tune
The sun has finally burst free

"Wake up, Inga!" Hanna nudged her fourteen-year-old sister, who was sleeping so soundly in her large wooden bed full of eiderdown quilts standing in the center of the room.

"Jag behöver inte vakna sig upp."

"No, no, today you must speak English," said Hanna as she tugged on the girl's blue flannel nightshirt.

It was true. Today was Thursday, and Inga's family spoke English on Thursdays to each other. Fru Anderson, their tutor, would soon be there to give the family English lessons.

"I don't want to wake up," said Inga again. But she raised quickly, poured water from the blue and white Chinese pitcher and washed her face in the matching china bowl on the washstand near her bed. Her toilet set had a matching toothbrush holder, soap dish, and commode, although with the new toilet on the first floor she seldom used the commode anymore. She smiled into the elegant oval mirror suspended by its harp over the triple-serpentine chest of the princess dresser and began to comb her long honey-blonde hair. She quickly braided it into one long rope that reached her waist. It was 6 a.m., and the chores must be finished before the guest arrived. On a large dairy farm, there were always chores to do.

"Will Fru Anderson bring us another surprise today?" asked Inga haltingly, remembering the American photo Fru Anderson had brought with her last week. It was a portrait of Fru Anderson in her wedding gown, taken in Chicago in 1885. The dress was white lace with puffy sleeves and a "train," as Fru Anderson had explained, of lace in the back, tied with a large bow at the waist. Her hair was swept up in a pile of black curls beneath a shoulder length veil. In her hands, she held a bouquet of orange blossoms with small orange fruit. How different it had looked from the Swedish weddings Inga had attended, where the couple dressed in traditional folk costumes and rode in a small, one-horse carriage with old shoes dragging in the dirt behind as they rode back to their farm to spend the night. Fru Anderson said that she and Herr Anderson had taken the train to a place called Niagara Falls, where she had purchased a postcard to remember the occasion.

"We'll have to see," said her older sister. "Come quickly. We must finish our chores before Fru Anderson arrives."

Inga made her bed neatly by straightening the eiderdown quilts and the heavy woolen and linen curtains on her tall, wooden enclosed Swedish bed that kept her warm in the frigid winters. She laid her French bisque doll on the pillow and straightened the doll's dress to cover the brown leather legs. Her large room included a sitting area, a small ceramic fireplace, a wardrobe, and a washstand and mirrored chest, all dimly lit by a small, curtained window. The housekeeper would soon come and dust, mop the floor, and empty the water bowl, but Inga straightened the tablecloth on the round table and neatly stacked the towels on the dry sink. Then she opened the heavy window drapes and let in the spring sunshine. She knew the house *tomten* would be pleased with her work. Even though she was fourteen, her mother often reminded her that brownies would not stay near a house that was messy. She hung her nightshirt on the hook behind the door, then slipped on a plain blouse and cotton skirt, along with some dark woolen stockings and painted soft-leather shoes before heading down the hallway to the back stairs and the privy in the porch. Later, she would put on her Sunday clothes for Fru Anderson.

She remembered the first time Fru Anderson had come to their farm. It was two years ago, just after Inga's older brothers had left for Canada. Because the farm would go to her oldest half-brother, the younger boys knew they would need to find work elsewhere. Per, the older, and Jan, the younger brother, had apprenticed themselves to carpenters in Ronneby, a town five miles east of Bräkne-Hoby, the closest town to their farm. Eventually, the two young men married two sisters from Bräkne-Hoby, and then sailed to Canada to homestead property northwest of Calgary. They had promised their wives that they would build a home and return for them, which they had. Both brothers' families lived in one tiny log cabin and would farm adjoining pieces of property until they could afford to build a second home. Papa had promised Per and Jan that the family would take English lessons and so Fru Anderson had been hired.

Fru Anderson was from Chicago, a large city in the United States that bordered the edge of the frontier. The whole city had burned in a fire in 1871, but now it was much larger than before. They had parks, a zoo, and shopping areas where you could buy everything under one roof. Men played a game called baseball, and many Swedish people had gone to Chicago to find jobs in the neighboring areas where trees were still abundant like Southern Sweden once had. Now, Sweden had open fields bordered by small areas of trees. It had all been logged before Inga was born because England needed the trees to build houses, factories, railroads, and businesses. They had purchased most of Sweden's trees for their Industrial Revolution, something that Sweden had yet to have. Men in the Chicago area usually worked in the lumber industry or house-building, while women found jobs as maids, secretaries, and factory workers. The women at Åskebode never tired of hearing Fru Anderson talk about Chicago. Herr Anderson, who was originally from Ronneby, had met Fru Anderson at the Svea Society, a social club for newly arrived Swedes and children of immigrants in the United States. Fru Anderson had been to secretary college and was earning her own wages when Herr Anderson convinced her to marry him and return to Sweden. Herr Anderson was Inga's schoolteacher from October through May, and Fru Anderson enjoyed the weekly visits to Inga's family because it was the only time she could speak English.

 Inga caught a whiff of strong black coffee and newly baked rye bread as she descended the back stairway to the kitchen. She slipped onto a bench under the wooden plank table as Hanna put clean dishes on a shelf above the sink and her mother dished a bowl of porridge for Inga.

 "You slept late," said Inga's mother as her hand pressed a wisp of graying hair back in place. "The men have already gone to the barn."

 Inga reached for a knife and butter for her bread. "I was tired today, are there any cucumbers or herring left?"

 "Yes, we saved you a piece of each, and here is your cereal."

 Inga carefully placed the cucumber slice and marinated fish on her rye bread and butter. The bowl of thick gruel, cooked from the grain of wheat and rye, steamed as her *mor* placed a pat of butter and a lump of brown sugar on top of it. This and a cup of strong coffee was a typical breakfast at the farmhouse for the family and hired hands.

 Inga took a spoonful of gruel and looked at her sister. Hanna was finishing the breakfast dishes using a large bucket of hot water from the stove on a side table where wet dishes were put into a tray with a dish rack, while Inga's mother rolled cookies for the morning tea on a smaller table. Times were not good in southern Sweden, where most farms fed the country. A drought had affected the farmland and agricultural products from the United States had flooded the local market at much lower prices than the locally grown items. Now no one seemed to be able to sell the little that they had grown. Only large farms such as Åskebode could make ends meet by selling veal, milk, and dairy products to the local townspeople and large amounts of cheese to the continent. Inga's family grew their own vegetables in a garden behind the house. Everything was canned in jars, pickled in barrows, or smoked in a small house behind the barn so they could eat all winter. In the kitchen, smoked sausage, fish, and meat hung with dried herbs from the ceiling waiting to be used in the fall when they could be stored in barrels for the winter.

While Inga ate her breakfast, Hanna came in with a bundle of flax from the barn. Every morning, she worked in the weaving room turning the flax into linen. The room was near the kitchen, so the wood stove with its cast iron top and sides would keep the most-used room warm in the winter. The stove was large with four big burners on top, a water reservoir, and a warming closet over the top. The two fire boxes below had to be fed every morning and restocked during the day. Below the fireboxes were ovens for cooking bread and rolls or a roast. A silver metal cord ran around the edge to hang pans, utensils, or sieves.

It took eleven steps and one entire year to make linen from the time it was planted in the spring until the linen was bleached in the sun the following year. Hanna had learned her profession from the *Folkhögskola* in Bräkne-Hoby. The school in Hoby was for learning agriculture, animal husbandry, and textiles. Hanna had lived there from October to May for two years to learn how to produce linen, weave textiles, and embroider in the style of traditional Swedish art. For the last year, she had been selling her work at stores in Ronneby. Hanna looked like a picture Inga had seen in a magazine. Her hair was pulled back in a thick, brown braid but the loose tendrils in front curled and wafted in the morning breeze, creating a soft halo around her head. Inga thought she looked beautiful with her plain cotton work blouse and striped cotton skirt full of flax shafts.

"*Hej*, Inga, would you please help me with the flax after you've finished your chores?" Before Inga could answer, Inga's *mor* walked through the doorway from the butler's pantry and said, "Not today, Hanna. I would like Inga to put out the coffee service in the parlor for Fru Anderson's visit. But first, Inga, you must feed your dog and cat before *Hustomten*, the house brownie complains about the service."

A wide smile crossed Inga's face at the reference to the *hustomten*. She put on a fresh white apron, rinsed her breakfast dishes, laid them on a rack, and then stopped at the door to take off her house shoes and slip on her wooden shoes before going out to feed Peeka, a hunting dog, and Strumpa, her cat, who had two white socks for paws. The animals waited impatiently at the back door while she cleaned their food dishes and spooned the breakfast leftovers into them. Then, after putting out a dish of water for the dog and some cream for the cat, she swept the porch so the *hustomten* would be pleased.

Talking to the elfin house brownie that she had never actually seen, Inga said, "I hope you like the way I've cleaned the porch, '*tomte*. Perhaps in return you'll bring me an *öre* so I can buy something when we go into town." Inga looked around at the neat yard where everything had its place. The wood was stacked in neat rows near the ornate smokehouse. The rain barrel stood at the end of the house where it caught soft water for their clothes and hair. The herb garden just outside the kitchen was starting to give signs of spring growth. Soon, small shoots of mustard, dill, caraway, parsley, sage, mint, and thyme would be basking in the sunshine. The family garden was weed-free. Two girls from town helped Inga's mother work in it every week from spring to late summer. They had just planted rows of lettuce, peas, beets, Swiss chard, potatoes, carrots, turnips, radishes, and cabbage and by the end of May they would be enjoying fresh vegetables again after the dark, cold winter. Inga looked around to make sure that the *hustomten* would like it. She knew that if the brownie was displeased, he would disappear and a troll would move in under the house. Trolls were known to steal children and replace them with their own kind. Everyone spoke of the *trollbarn,* children who lived in the house down the road. The children fought, the parents yelled, and the house and garden were a mess. No *hustomten* lived there! Inga always looked carefully at the children in that house when she passed. It was hard to tell a troll child. They could look just like humans when they wanted, but by themselves they were dirty, had straw-like messy hair, warty noses, and a cow's tail hung down their backs. Inga had heard mothers whisper that someone in Hoby had had a child that was stolen by a troll when it was born. The troll child was ugly and deformed so the parents had set the child out-of-doors in winter just after it was born and the trolls had taken it back. Another time, a fourteen-year-old boy had argued with his parents and, that night, the boy disappeared into the woods. Trolls got him for sure. *Mor* said it was because he didn't respect his parents and didn't say the Lord's Prayer on the way to the woods after dark. He was never seen again.

    Looking towards the barn, Inga saw the hired hands herding the black and white cows out to pasture. They had just finished milking and, as the sun rose in the east, daylight brought vibrant colors to the small valley where she lived. The rich green meadow surrounding her home contrasted with the dusty road that wound its way in front of her house and over the River Vierydsån in front of the low hills. The road and the river then continued south toward the sea, which was just half a mile away. Seagulls, snow geese, and wild swans were often seen flying overhead. Because the Vierydsån River was deep, smaller seafaring boats often sailed up stream as far as the village, which was really just a cluster of houses on the edge of the water one half mile from Åskebode. The beach at Vierydsån was a place where the community swam. The entire neighborhood would enjoy themselves with the cool water, small boat launches, and diving platforms. Children under the age of twelve usually swam naked, and often their parents did also if no one else was around. After a long winter, people longed for the rays of the sun to warm their skin after a cool swim. The Vierydsån continued north to a small waterfall and large boulders, then wound its way to a small lake called Salsjö which was closer to the town of Bräkne-Hoby.

Inga's thoughts returned to her responsibilities as she saw her *mor* setting a potted red geranium out-of-doors in the spring sunshine. Inga put the broom away and left her wooden shoes on a bench by the back door. Walking in her stocking feet, she stepped inside and slipped back into her house slippers and began gathering the items she would need for serving refreshments from the butler's pantry. First, she selected a beautiful white linen tablecloth with matching napkins to cover the tea table in the parlor. Then, she carefully lifted the large silver coffee pot, and the tiny ornate cream and sugar bowl onto the serving tray. After, she chose four pale green Meissen china cups, saucers, and dessert plates with pale green and white leaves and small purple and gold grapes painted on the sides to match the gold trim around the edges. Finally, she selected four tiny silver teaspoons. Inga made several trips to the parlor so she wouldn't drop anything until all that was left was the placement of the napkins. She looked closely at the four napkins made of linen woven by her sister, Hanna. On each border, her sister had embroidered tiny pink and blue flowers and green oak leaves, which represented Blekinge, the county where Ronneby and Bräkne-Hoby were located. She marveled at her sister's handiwork. Hanna, seven years older than

Inga, was very adept at sewing and she had been teaching Inga to do it as well. Last winter, Inga had woven a cloth of linen on the handloom all by herself. This winter, she would make a sampler of all the stitches she had learned for her mother's birthday gift. Inga remembered the large hand-woven linen wall cloth in a trunk in her mother's room. It had been made by her mother's great-grandmother in the 1700s and was considered a museum piece. It was twenty-six feet long and five feet wide, and decorated with geometric patterns of blue on white. Inga saw it only during *Julfest*, at Christmastime, when it was hung horizontally around the living room wall. It was called an *Överhogdal* tapestry, and her *mor's mormor* had traveled to Brussels to be trained in the art of tapestry to make it perfect.

Inga stepped back to take one last look at the parlor. The heavy wooden furniture shone like glass, and Inga could see herself in the legs of the chairs as they curved to the floor like a swan's neck. The heavy-cut velvet upholstery contrasted nicely with the white linen tablecloth and silver coffee service. *Lagom ä bäst*, thought Inga, just right is best. The petite settee and matching arm and side chairs with their spindle backs and cabriole legs curved delicately to the floor. Behind them stood a grandfather clock, an English Chippendale block front desk, and, in the corner, a cylindrical ceramic fireplace stood in which her *mor* had started a fire to keep the chill off the room. On the walls were oil paintings of her grandparents, the city of Stockholm, and a lake which Inga had never seen in person but she knew wasn't too far away; small *stugas* were built around it by people from Stockholm with money. A plate rail ran around the room over the top of tongue-and-groove paneling; five feet off the ground, the rail held pewter chargers for fancy dinners, and in the south-facing windows, geraniums were starting to bloom as the spring sun shone through the wavy glass. Rag rugs woven by Inga's mother covered some of the wooden floor. Not formal, but certainly not folksy, the room was Inga's favorite.

In the weaving room, Hanna was busy carding flax. It was the eighth step in the process of making linen. Hanna had planted the flax seed last spring, and when it had reached its full height, the family had helped her pull it up by the roots to allow for the longest possible fibers. It was then tied into bundles and hung up to dry in the barn. By the end of summer, the dried bundles were washed in the river that ran near the farm and set on the bank to dry. The husks had rotted. Finally, after a few days of drying on the hillside, the flax was ready to be scraped. This meant laying the flax between a pair of wooden knives that removed the remaining outer husks. After the fibers were ready, the rest of the work could be done during the winter in the barn or the house, when the days were dark, the temperature below zero, and crunchy white snow lay on the ground. Hanna was now combing, or carding, the flax with spiked boards, which straightened the fibers in preparation for spinning them into threads. This would be done on the spinning wheel. Afterwards, it would be woven into beautiful cloth on the six-foot-high loom off the kitchen. So many steps were necessary before the finished product could be enjoyed. Inga knew why Hanna was paid well by the merchants who bought the linen. She walked over to the piece she had woven last winter and wondered if she would ever be as good as Hanna at weaving.

Hanna was gazing out the window towards the barn while she carded flax. She was watching Henry Thorsell, a farm hand who had been with the family for eight years. His back glistened in the sunshine as he caught hay from the upper floor of the barn and placed it into a wagon to distribute to the cows. Hanna told Inga she had dreamed of Henry several times, even though she was twenty-one and he was only twenty, but through the years he never seemed to notice her. He was over six feet tall and muscular, and his shaggy brown hair and handlebar mustache blew in the light breeze from the sea. His baggy button-waist pants with their leather suspenders hanging down couldn't hide the fact that he was very strong. His long muscular legs complimented two arms that looked like oak trees from working on a farm since he was a boy. The hair on his chest glistened with sweat as he worked in the morning sun. Though he bunked in the barn with the other farm hands and came into the main house only for meals, Hanna knew where he was every minute of the day. She never talked to him directly, but often heard her father and the workers talking in the kitchen. She especially listened for Henry's lilting Swedish voice. He had only been homeschooled for five years, but he read his Bible every night in the light of the oil lamp in the barn where he bunked to practice his reading. He was always polite and helped her into the carriage when the family and farm hands went to church on Sundays, but he spoke only to the men, keeping his eyes to the ground when Hanna was around. He realized he was the hired hand and she was the owner's daughter, a position that would be permanent in Sweden. Hanna knew that most poor men didn't marry until they were in their thirties. They had to save every bit of money they earned in order to buy a small piece of land with a house, and then they married young girls who were sixteen to eighteen years old. Hanna was already considered an old maid among her friends, who had all married. The older men were already looking at girls younger than her for their wives. Hanna sighed deeply and turned to find Inga looking at Henry also.

Noticing that Hanna was watching her, Inga quickly moved away and looked down at the cloth in her hands.

"Hanna, when will we set my piece of cloth out in the sunshine to be bleached?" asked Inga.

"Soon," Hanna answered. *"En svala gör ingen sommar.* One swallow does not mean it is summer. But the days are growing longer now and I will set out many pieces along with yours, when I know it will not rain." Inga compared hers to those that Hanna had made last winter. Hers had many flaws and was uneven where the weft had not been tight enough, but it was a major project for her.

She laid her piece among the others as the clock in the parlor struck 9:30. Fru Anderson would be there in half an hour.

"Fru Anderson will be here soon," said Hanna, looking at the dried flax on her clothing. "We had better start getting ready."

Inga walked with her to the front stairs and looked up to see that the housekeeper had changed into her better clothes in anticipation of Fru Anderson's arrival. She had been on the porch earlier, where she had washed yesterday's clothes and hung them out to dry; she would iron them later this afternoon. She worked hard alongside the family members. In addition to the large house with its eight bedrooms, the barn had sleeping quarters for the five ranch hands that stayed on the farm all year around. But on a farm, everyone had to work hard from sunup to sundown to get the work done, or there wouldn't be enough food or supplies for the long, dark Swedish winters. On December 21st, the day was only two hours long in southern Sweden where Inga lived, and the sun shined not at all in northern Sweden for three months.

This was the reason Per and Jan had decided to go to Canada when they found the farm would not stay in their family. The territory known as Alberta, Canada, had climate and daylight similar to that of southern Sweden. In Sweden, a family farm always went to the first son, or daughter if there were no sons. The farm legally belonged to Karl Olof. But over the years, he and his stepfather could not agree on how it should be run, so when Karl was eighteen years old he had left Åskeboda with only a note to his mother. They hadn't heard from him since.

Per and Jan had married their wives in a double wedding six weeks after posting their engagements at the Bräkne-Hoby Lutheran church. They had been seeing the girls at dances and social functions and Per had danced and walked in the woods with Mina on *Midsommer's Eve*. The night was only two hours long so teenagers generally stayed out all night after the folk festival. Eight weeks later, Per announced that he and Mina had decided to marry. Jan and Edla soon made the same decision and both couples began *natt frieri*, or bundling. Inga had asked her mother about bundling and was told that the boy and girl were allowed to sleep together in the girl's home, but they were fully clothed and not allowed to touch. The girl stayed under the covers and the boy stayed on top, or a wooden board was placed between them. This gave the couple time to talk and make plans for their future. After the weddings, the brothers went to Canada, built a small house, and returned a year later to collect their wives and Per's young son.

Inga and Hanna moved to the side as the housekeeper came down the stairs, then they made their way to their bedrooms. Inga noticed that the housekeeper had been in her room. The water on the washstand had been replaced, the wooden floors dry-mopped, and fresh clothes hung in the wardrobe. Inga pulled out the drawers beneath her bed and found a silk petticoat and white stockings; from the wardrobe she got a crisp white linen blouse with a large collar. Her *mor* had hand-embroidered white flowers on the collar. Hanging also in her wardrobe was a new pink and blue striped skirt that her *mor* had recently finished. She sat on her small bedroom chair and pulled on her white stockings and soft leather slippers. While lacing them, she glanced around the room at its white walls, pink stenciled flowers, and linen wall hangings, wondering what new words they would learn that day. She unbraided her hair and divided it into two halves. Braiding each side tightly, she pinned it across the top of her head as the older girls did. She wished it was summer so she could put some flowers in her hair, but settled on bright ribbons that matched her skirt. Last, she put on a starched linen apron with traditional Blekinge embroidery around the bottom. Looking in the mirror, she smiled at her reflection. She looked like a miniature of Hanna on Sundays and hoped the others would notice. After all, she had laid out the silver service today without help from her mother.

She quickly walked down the hall and reached the top of the stairs when a soft knock was heard at the door. Inga's mother and Hanna were there to meet Fru Anderson. Inga stepped confidently down the stairs as the others turned to see her. Fru Anderson winked at Inga as Inga looked down into Fru Anderson's hands. In them lay a copy of *Heart and Home*, which had just arrived from the United States.

As Inga glanced out of the front door, Henry Thorsell had come from the barn. He had been transferring fresh milk into large five gallon buckets to be taken to the cheese factory in Ronneby. Instead, he began to lead Fru Anderson's cabriolet and horse to the barn, where he would water and feed the horse some hay. He would then unhook it from the carriage and lead it into a stall to rest.

She remembered how he came to live with her family when he was twelve years old while his parents lived a few miles from the sea, in Karlsham, west of Bräkne-Hoby. His father was a poor fisherman and small ship builder, his mother sewed garments for a local store, and his smaller brothers and sisters had not learned trades yet. They lived in a one-room fisherman's cottage and the kids slept up in the loft. The children were home schooled and would learn to read from the Bible, but Henry had learned through the years that education was not needed for most farm jobs; what was important was having manners, being polite, dressing cleanly, and being on time. The Ola Nilsson family had been like his own as he lived, worked, and ate on their farm. Ola was a good employer unless he was gambling or drinking. Henry adored Hanna and her sister Inga, but missed the older boys when they moved to Canada with their wives.

CHAPTER 2
June 1889

Dance around the bonfire
And raise the Maypole high
Then meet me in our secret place
To watch the stars go by
The crops have all been planted
St. Olof's Day comes soon
So meet me in our secret place
To dance around the moon

The farm hands packed the wagon full of food while Inga's family got ready for the *Midsommerfest*. They had already decorated the doorway of the house and barn with branches of green leaves and young birch trees on each side of the entrances. Inside the house, the six fireplaces were fronted with fresh, green foliage and vases of wild flowers were on every table. Everyone was dressed in traditional summer folk costumes. The women wore striped aprons over dark skirts and starched white-linen blouses that were tight from the elbow to the wrist and embroidered at the collar. Over these, they wore blue vests embellished with embroidery that had carved animal bone or silver buttons. White triangular scarves with flowers of Blekinge embroidered on them covered part of their hair, and matching scarves went around their shoulders and were knotted below silver brooches encrusted with stones or jewels. In their hair were carved combs decorated with scrimshaw and silver barrettes with traditional animal decoration and ribbon filigree. At their waists hung small, square embroidered purses that contained things that Vikings carried: a wooden spoon and fork, a handkerchief, a small steel dagger with a carved wooden handle and two inch blade secured in a leather case, small rune stones with ancient Viking writing, and a few *öre* to play games or buy treats made by the church auxiliary. White woolen stockings of thin yarn reached their knees under their skirts. On their feet were either black leather shoes with silver buckles or wooden shoes decorated with *rosemaling*. All of the traditional clothing had been made years ago when Inga's grandmother had been alive, but was lovingly kept for holidays and special events.

The men wore dark woolen knickers that were embroidered with traditional emblems in the front and around the sides of the legs. Their thin white stockings were held at the knee by garters with red tassels on the sides. Crisp white long-sleeved shirts were topped with bright red vests that had two rows of silver buttons down the front. Tight around their necks were red bowties that stuck out over their collars, giving their tan faces a red glow. A sheath at their waist carried their eating implements and their daggers.

The weather cooperated on this special day as white cotton clouds drifted over without raining. The sun, which had risen at 1 a.m., would not set until 11 p.m., twenty-two hours later. It was the shortest night of the year, and a special one for lovers in Sweden.

Inga looked forward to seeing her schoolmates. She hadn't seen some of them since the end of April when school had let out for planting. *Midsommerfest* was one of the few celebrations they had during the busy summer. It had started as a pagan holiday of the ancient Vikings who worshipped the sun, but was later adopted by the Lutheran church as a holiday to celebrate John the Baptist. In Bräkne-Hoby, everyone gathered at the *Folkhögskola*, the school gymnasium, as it was the only place large enough to hold the townspeople in case the weather turned to rain.

Everyone was excited about the holiday. Inga's *mor* had baked pies of *lingonberries* that Inga had picked along the river's edge. They also made apple, pear, and nut pies. There were sausages and smoked meats to slice and take with them. Then there were rolls, bread, herring, pickled eggs, potato salad, cabbage rolls, and smoked pink salmon for the *smorgasbord*. Only Inga's father, Ola, was not around to enjoy the outing. He had gone to England on business and, unfortunately, would not be back in time.

Just before leaving the farm, Inga ran up to her mother's bedroom. The night before, she had a dream and she wanted to ask her mother about it.

"*Mor,* can I talk to you for a minute?" asked Inga, out of breath from climbing the stairs.

"Of course," answered Inga's mother. "I was just remembering a *Midsommerfest* thirty-five years ago where I met my first husband." Inga's *mor*, Bertha, looked at the rocking chair in her bedroom. Her dead husband, Michael, had made it the year they were married. Inga knew her mother rocked in the chair and sometimes talked low to herself. Once in a while, she heard the name, Michael, as if her mother were actually speaking to him.

Inga knew that Michael had drowned off the coast of Denmark in a terrible storm. Denmark was a country stuck between two oceans that vented their fury on the islands and peninsula. Taking a ship from Sweden to Denmark was the only way to get to the continent, and the ships must pass through the channels of the Skager Rack and Cattegat. The ships that passed between the islands were tossed within a labyrinth of channels like the tentacles of a sea monster. While miles of strong, shifting currents called each ship to their doom, hundreds of lighthouses and lightships lit the way. Besides the fogs and reefs, the winds were so fierce that no one lived along the coast. When a ship was called to destruction, little could be done for it.

Her mother said he was a *gast*, a soul without a Christian burial that still walked the world because of unfinished business. Inga had lived all her life with ghosts, although she had never actually seen one. Her mother talked to Grandma Anna like she was still in the room, and she talked to Michael, too, when Ola, her second husband, wasn't around. Inga figured that losing the two most important people in her mother's life all in the same year had caused her mother's mind to see what others could not.

To Inga, ghosts seemed natural. They were no different than *hustomtens*, who took care of the house, farm, and animals, and warned the farmer with a gentle nudge if danger was around. The *tomten* was the last one to retire at night and always made sure that all the doors were locked and that the lamps and candles were out. Everyone wanted a *tomten* around. Then there were trolls who wanted to be human. They feared man and often turned into logs or boulders when men were around. They lived under the roots of trees, or in caves and hollows and sometimes houses if they possessed a human. They hid their loot of silver, gold, and things stolen from human beings. *Skogsra* lived in the forest and were wood nymphs that were beautiful on the outside and lured men to their beds, but their backs and brains were hollowed out and empty. Inga had never seen them, so why not a *gast* or *spoke*? Many older Swedes would tell stories of those who had died and who would *gå igen*, or reappear after death.

Inga looked at her mother's face. Her hair was almost white, although she was only fifty years old, but her skin was as unwrinkled as when she was twenty.

"*Mor*, can I ask you about a dream I had last night?"

Bertha looked deeply into Inga's eyes and made the sign of a cross to avert the devil. "What have you seen in your dreams?" she asked nervously as she sat down to rock.

"I saw a man that I have seen many times in my dreams, but I don't know who he is," said Inga.

"What did this man look like?"

"He looks very kindly, with blond hair and ruddy skin. He wears thick glasses and is slightly stooped. He always says the same thing," replied Inga.

Bertha's eyes had widened at the description and breathlessly she asked, "What is it he says?"

"He always says, 'Åskeboda is lost,' then his eyes fill with tears as he turns away and walks toward the barn," said Inga.

Inga's mother nodded her head in understanding. She sighed a heavily and continued to rock. "*Döden är vår Herres sopkvast.* Death is our Lord's broom. You have the sight," she said softly.

"What sight, *Mor*?"

"You are *De Kloka*, a wise one, like your grandmother. The man you saw in your dream was my Michael trying to warn me of the future."

Inga tried to understand her mother's words. *De Klocka* was a term used to describe either a wise one or a witch who comes from *Blåkulla*, the mountains in the north. Which one was she to be?

"Inga, do not tell anyone what you have told me. It will only bring you unhappiness in life like your Grandma Anna. *Otack ä värdens iön.* The world's reward is ingratitude."

"Was Grandma Anna a witch?" asked Inga, her hands shaking.

"No. My mother had the sight, but when she tried to warn people of things she had dreamed, they called her names. You must never tell anyone you have it. It will only cause problems for you. Do not try to change your fate. Let life unfold the way God intended."

With that, Bertha kissed her daughter's forehead and told her to be ready for the *Midsommerfest* in a few minutes. They would enjoy themselves no matter what the future held.

Inga was very quiet as the wagon took the women and farm hands to Bräkne-Hoby. She sat wondering how many dreams she would have that foretold the future. Did every dream contain a message, or only some of them? How was she to know which ones to believe? Her eyes were caught by the sight of a large moose drinking from the river. As the wagon crossed over the old wooden bridge, she turned her attention to the passing pastoral scenes. The birch trees swayed in the breeze and robins followed the slow-moving wagon, looking for bugs kicked up in the dust. As the wagon turned left and passed *Hjälmseryd* farm, old Fru Pehrsdotter and her son waved as they too climbed into their wagons to attend the festival. The road turned south for half a mile and then paralleled the sea, where Inga caught a glimpse of giant white swans and their cygnets swimming close to shore. The wagon continued on the dirt road, winding through stands of birch, oak, hawthorn, and poplars, and past large fields of rye, wheat, and vegetables. Orchards of apples, pears, and cherries were promising a good harvest. Luckily, the farmers were not as destitute as those who lived in the city, but there still was not enough land to buy or jobs to be had for those who lived in Sweden. Inga had read about factories and industries that gave England and the United States prosperity, but Sweden was many years from having its own factories and government businesses.

An hour later, the wagon passed Bräkne-Hoby Church and the parson's house with its red siding and white window trim. The town's people began to form a long line of wagons up the narrow lane to the *Folkhögskola* property. Inga looked at the homes that had stood in Bräkne-Hoby for as long as anyone could remember. Some were large, stately, and fashioned after houses from the continent. These were on the *Folkhögskola* property and were occupied by professors and teachers, people who had traveled and seen the world. Others were small and folksy and belonged to small farmers and businessmen. But all of them were neat and well cared for in hopes that a *hustomten* would come and stay. The woodpiles were stacked perfectly, and the smokehouses were decorated with *rosemaling* and carved with ancient symbols. Ironwork decorated the corner of each loft, and sod roofs covered many structures. Each yard had a small garden for the owner's fresh vegetables. Inga smiled as she noticed a rabbit or two in each yard.

As the wagon slowly climbed the hill to the large school, Inga began to hear the first strains of a local band warming up for the folk dancing. In the center of the grass, strong men raised the Maypole, which was decorated with ivy garlands and colorful ribbons. On the top, it was trimmed with small sailboats that hung from the crossbar to promise the fishermen good catches at sea. She looked at Hanna and the other women chatting and waving at a few friends within calling distance as the wagon plodded along. Inga realized that she had had a dream about Hanna and Henry Thorsell, the farm hand. Looking at the two of them, she began to see that, although the two ignored each other, there was a certain magnetism that she hadn't noticed before. Would Hanna and Henry marry? Inga longed to know, but remembered her mother's warning. "Don't try to change fate, let nature take its course." That's what she would do.

As the wagon pulled up to the *Folkhögskola*, the men jumped out of the wagon as it stopped and helped the women down from the back. Inga saw that Hanna's hand held Henry's a little longer than necessary, but he didn't seem to notice.

Inga helped take the many dishes of food over to the long tables bedecked with wild flowers and garlands of fresh green foliage. Everyone had brought something, whatever they could afford, and the women from Åskeboda had brought the most. The school had set tables and chairs around the grass area and the band played on the wide entrance steps that led to the second floor. Two fiddlers and an accordionist began to warm up as a double circle of dancers gathered around the Maypole.

Inga loved the school with its ivy-covered walls and white columns. She turned around to look at the familiar houses along the road that they had come up and the train station situated in the middle of town. Farther west, she could just catch sight of the small harbor at Järnavik and the sea beyond. She was sure that if she hadn't smelled the good food and sweet honeysuckle growing up on the hill, she would have smelled the fresh clean scent of the ocean breeze. Around the school were fields of grain used by the students and faculty to develop better strains of wheat, barley, rye, and flax. The long gravel lane was lined with fruit trees of all kinds and a long row of brightly colored tree roses. The four-story building full of classrooms and laboratories also included a cafeteria for students who boarded. To the west was another building with dormitory rooms, each one big enough for a bed and a closet for every student.

Inga looked down the lane to the beautiful white church with its tall steeple rising above the trees. She had spent nearly every Sunday in that church for as long as she could remember, and every deceased member of her family was buried in the surrounding cemetery. Although the church looked small on the outside, upon entering the ceilings rose like an upside-down ship's hull, painted white and decorated with biblical paintings and pictures of the life of Christ and Saints of the Lutheran church. Inside were rows of wooden pews and boxed pews for prominent families which stood closer to the pulpit. The church and town were near and dear to Inga's heart.

If Åskeboda was lost, where would she and her family go? What would they do? She wished that she could see into the future and know how it would turn out. She heard the melancholy call of the train as it pulled into the station. Friends from Karlshamn and Ronneby and beyond would be coming to the country festival where traditions were kept and where a feeling of stability and roots were felt among the people. It was a family reunion at its best. Neighbor visited neighbor and family visited family to hear the news of the last year. Here, friends became lovers and those gone were remembered, and the youth were taught traditions that had been here for hundreds, if not thousands, of years.

As the musicians began the first *Schottische,* Inga ran to join the group in hopes that someone needed a partner. She looked up to see her mother smiling at her. Nodding to the beat of the music, Inga's thoughts turned to Michael, the kindly man in her dreams, and she knew why her mother missed him so.

An old man next to her called to his granddaughter, who was walking down the path to Salsjö, the lake in the woods. "Stay near the school, Britta," he warned. Then to his wife he muttered, "*Midsommer* night is not long, but it sets many a cradle rocking." Inga looked at the Maypole of ivy and flowers and sang the traditional *Midsommer* song with others:

Uti vår hage, Där växa blå bar	*From out of spring pastures the blueberries grow*
Kom hjärtens fröd	*Come heartfelt joy*
Vill du mig något	*Do you feel the same,*
Så träffas vi där	*then come greet we there*
Kom, liljor och akveleja	*Come lilies and daisies*
Kom, rosor ach salivia	*Come roses and Salvia*
Kom ljuva, krusmynta	*Come sweet mint*
Kom, hjӓrtens fröld!	*Come heartfelt joy*

It was after 2 p.m. when Inga decided to take a break from serving food. She found her girlfriend Karin wiping the perspiration from her forehead and drinking a cool glass of ale.

"How about going with me to Salsjö? I could use a sauna and a dip in the lake," said Inga.

"Me too," replied Karin. "But I need to help clean up. I promised my *mor*. Why don't you go down and save us a spot and I'll bring sandwiches and some ale for later? I shouldn't be more than half an hour."

"That would be great," Inga replied. "I'll take a blanket from the back of our wagon and see you there."

As Inga walked over to the wagon and picked up a blanket and towel, several young men Hanna had been with at school were talking and laughing. As she walked by, one said, "Inga, want to go swimming with us?"

Inga looked at them curiously. The boys had been drinking.

"No, thanks. I'm going to wait for Karin." She started down the path from the school. It wound through some professors' homes and into a thick stand of trees. It would take twenty minutes of walking to get to Salsjö. She stopped at a small stream where a rock had been hollowed out by ancient Vikings and sipped a handful of cool, clean water. The group of men she had talked to passed by and several made some crude remarks. She ignored them and wondered why they were acting like schoolboys when some were in their early twenties.

She let them get well ahead of her before continuing on her way. In the silence that followed, Inga saw animals peeking out of their hiding places to see if they were alone. A hedgehog ran across the path looking for snails and slugs to eat. A deer stepped deeper into the woods. Inga thought of the many times she had taken this path while attending the *Midsommerfest*. She crossed the dirt road and followed the path that skirted a small pond. The mosquitoes were thick in the air. Inga fought her way through the swarms by closing her eyes and flailing her arms. When she opened them, there stood the boys in front of her.

"Inga, need some help with those mosquitoes?" asked Bjorn.

"No," answered Inga as she tried to step around him.

"How about us escorting you to the lake?" said Tomas.

"No, thanks," replied Inga, trying her best to ignore the men.

Bjorn grabbed Inga's blanket and taunted her with it, walking backwards in front of her.

"How about you and me using the blanket?" said Bjorn.

Inga began to panic. There were three of them and only one of her, and not another person on the trail.

"Keep it," said Inga as she tried to walk faster. But the boys were not going to let her go. They began to touch her arms and her hair, pulling off her scarf and grabbing the combs that held her hair together. Her hair began to fall from the top of her head and to unbraid itself. Inga turned in circles trying to watch each of the boys, but as she turned, the one behind her would grab at her clothing.

"*Djävular!* Devils! Leave me alone!" she exclaimed. But the men were becoming excited at the game they played. Finally, one grabbed her from behind and threw her over his shoulder, racing into the woods with the other two close behind. Inga let out a yell hoping that someone would hear, but a hand clamped over her mouth as her head began to spin.

When she awoke, she lay on the ground with her vest and blouse unbuttoned. The scarf and broach had been tossed onto a bush. Her hair lay disheveled over her budding breasts. One boy held both arms and one had his hand over her mouth as the other stood at her feet. Bjorn knelt down and slowly pushed her skirt and petticoat up to her waist as he knelt between her legs and started to pull down his pants.

"Don't fight it, Inga," he muttered excitedly, looking down at her. Inga's eyes shut tight as she waited for the worst to happen.

Suddenly, she heard the crashing of branches then a heavy thud as Bjorn was knocked from above her. She opened her eyes to see Henry Thorsell land a kick to Bjorn's stomach and as he fell backwards, Henry slammed a fist into his mouth. As Bjorn recovered from the unexpected blows, the two men scuffled into the bushes. Bjorn landed several blows to Henry's face and then they both rolled in the dirt. Henry held Bjorn's chest tight for several seconds, squeezing the air out of him. When he let go, Bjorn coughed and went limp in Henry's arms. As Henry stood up, the other boys scattered and ran.

It was several moments before Inga realized that she was free. She covered her face with her hands and began to sob. Now that the nightmare was over, she was shaking like a leaf.

Henry called to the men that fled, "*Dra ät häklefjäl!* I'll see you in hell!" Then he kneeled and gently began to cover Inga with her blanket.

"I'm sorry, Inga. I'm so sorry I didn't get here sooner."

"*Tack*. Thank you, Henry," was all that she could think of to say as he took her in his arms and gently rocked her.

Later, when the crying had stopped and she had dressed and regained her composure, Inga leaned heavily on Henry's arm as they walked to Salsjö. She wanted to cleanse herself in the cold water of the lake and scrub the hands of the boys from her body. Together, they found a secluded patch of grass and each of them slipped off their heavy costumes and wrapped themselves in towels. Walking toward the small boat dock, Henry saw bruises on Inga's arms and was disgusted with himself for not seeing her trouble before he did.

Inga dropped her towel and dove into the cold, icy water near the small dam and Henry followed her, not permitting himself to touch her after all that had happened. She had had enough manhandling for the day. They were still swimming when Karin arrived with sandwiches and ale. Inga stepped up the ladder, water dripping from her cooled skin, and walked to the end of the pier where her towel lay. Slowly, she wrapped the towel around her and looked at Karin. As she turned to Henry, he said, "Go with your friend. I'm going to take a sauna."

Inga looked at him and smiled weakly.

"*Tack*," she whispered again, and turned towards Karin, who was taking the sandwiches and ale out of the basket. Henry nodded slightly and smiled a little, wondering if Inga would ever tell anyone what had happened. Soon others arrived to swim and sauna. She and Karin ate the small lunch, swam, and then walked back to the *Folkhögskola*.

At 11 p.m., the sun dipped below the horizon, and a hushed silence came over the woods. It was s*kymning*, twilight. The birds stopped singing, the owls began to hoot, and the night flowers burst forth with the heady scent of gardenias and jasmine. It was the time of night when midsummer cast its spell on lovers. At the *Folkhögskola*, the teenagers moved into the darkness as their parents began to clean up the dishes and pack the food. Lovers strolled arm in arm, and others talked quietly under the trees as the band put away their instruments. Horses were bridled for the long trip home, and strong coffee was made for those who waited for the train. Girls who were unattached walked to a nearby meadow where a bouquet of seven kinds of flowers were picked to place under their pillow in hopes of dreaming of the man they would marry.

Within two hours, the night was over, the sun once again came over the horizon, and the last of the partygoers began their journey home. Hanna, asleep in her mother's arms, laid in the back of the wagon. The farm hands nodded their heads while humming a tune from the night before. Only Henry and Inga sat quietly at opposite ends of the wagon, each in their own thoughts about the happenings of the day. As the wagon made the one-hour trip home, the two young people occasionally glanced at each other but not a word was said.

Henry yawned as he trotted the horses back to Åskeboda. It had been a long day and he was just getting home in time to start the milking of the cows. He would try and get a cat nap sometime between his chores. *Midsommerfest* was a national holiday, so he knew that many farm workers would be dragging themselves around while the farm owners and their families slept until noon. He thought about the future and realized that he would be saving money for years before he could buy some land or small house. He could go back to Karlsham where his father and mother lived, but they really could not afford to feed him unless he wanted to eat fresh fish half the year and dried fish the other half. No, he preferred to live on a farm, even if it was not his own.

Thinking of the rich boys who played mean games with the girls, not thinking of the consequences of their actions, and knowing that Inga would never tell her parents what they had done to frighten her, Henry knew being rich let the kids get away with much more than those who were poor. Would things ever change? The rich kids could rely on their parents to get them out of trouble by paying off a government official or local sheriff, while the poor kids were blamed for wrongdoing and sent to jail.

CHAPTER 3
June 1889

The cows have returned with their calves from the hills
The leaves now turn orange and red
Women of Sweden their creameries fill
For the day to make cheese is ahead
Women of Sweden their creameries fill
For the day to make cheese is ahead

Inga and the women of Åskeboda sat in the big farm wagon driven by Henry Thorsell. Among the women were kettles and containers of milk for the *Ystmote,* or cheesemaking, being held at Hjälmseryd. As the wagon pulled up to the barn-style house, Inga noticed four other wagons had already arrived. Henry helped each woman out of the wagon and then began unloading the milk and placing it outside the front door. Soon girls came and began to dip into the containers and take quantities of milk into the house to be boiled.

"That's far enough, Henry," Inga's *mor* warned. "We don't want you to spoil the cheese by you getting too close to the stoop."

Henry nodded and then reminded Bertha that he would be back at 4 p.m. to pick the women up.

Inga was excited to be there. She had never been allowed to attend the cheesemaking before. The women didn't have time to tend children because the work was hot and exacting and Inga always had to watch the younger children at a different farm before. She remembered part of a dream about Hjälmseryd and knew she had been there before, but she had never been inside. The owner of Hjälmseryd, a woman in her seventies named Fru Pehrsdotter, had an unmarried son. She was the best cheesemaker in the county and everyone looked forward to being invited to her home to make it.

Each family brought enough milk and cream to make a portion of cheese that would last their family for a year. Cheesemaking was women's work. The men were not allowed inside for fear their presence would disturb the influences, curdling the milk and spoiling its coagulation. The same happened with butter. No butter would appear until the men left the house. After the milk was boiled in great kettles, rennet was added to start the coagulation. The juice was squeezed out of the lumpy material and then pressed into wooden forms.

Inga looked around the property at Hjälmseryd. A small building was close to the street. It had once been a house with a Dutch door and one large room and had been occupied by people for over one hundred years, but now it served as a pig barn. It had a worn dirt floor and a loft in the roof that had once been for sleeping. Two windows had been on the front side of the house, but now they were boarded up to keep out the rain and snow. Birch trees surrounded the small house and ivy climbed the walls. Inga could see that the roof was coming off in places where the filtered sun shone through.

The new house, built in 1869, was in the shape of a barn. It was two stories high with red siding and white window trim. The two windows beside the front door were unusual. Inga had never seen an entry like it before. The front door opened onto a thick, green lawn instead of a porch because most people used the back door, where they could take off their shoes when they entered the house. The south side of the house was full of windows, even tiny ones at the corners of the eaves, to capture the sun in the winter. Between the houses was a well for water that was probably original and a path that led to the river. It was the same small river that ran near Inga's home and into the Salsjö two miles north.

Inga stepped cautiously through the door, not knowing what to expect.

"Come in, child," said Fru Pehrsdotter sweetly. "Grab a pitcher for milk and take it to the kitchen."

Inga picked up a pitcher, filled it with milk from the kettle and walked back through the house. As she passed the parlor, she saw beautiful dark furniture, a grand piano in the corner, and green plants hung everywhere and standing in front of the windows. The tables were covered with crisp white linen, and hand-tatted lace covered the backs and arms of overstuffed chairs. The cream-colored walls had large paintings and tapestries hanging by dark ribbons. By the time she had made twenty trips, she could remember everything in the room.

"*Mor*," said Inga to her mother after several trips, "can I rest a bit?"

"Many hands make light work," replied Bertha. As the women boiled the milk, Fru Pehrsdotter watched each pot, carefully adjusting the coals in the old stoves.

"Stir a little faster," Fru Pehrsdotter said to a girl perspiring over a kettle. "I'm going to add the rennet soon."

At another kettle, the milk was beginning to coagulate into lumps. Nearby, a woman was pressing a large lump into a loosely-woven cloth so the moisture would drain away. At a table, two women were pressing the cheese into wooden forms to cool.

"Take a short break, Inga," said Fru Pehrsdotter. "We'll need you to get more milk soon."

Inga set her pitcher down and walked into the parlor she had passed so many times. She looked at the overstuffed chairs with wooden arms and legs that shone in the midmorning sun. The round table between them had small pieces of wood inlaid on the top and gentle curving legs. Inga had never seen such beautiful furniture. The grand piano in the corner had a lace tablecloth across it and on the top were many daguerreotypes of people. She looked from one to another until she found a portrait of women in her twenties. Her brown hair was pinned back with a part down the middle and her blouse had a high button collar with gently curving ruffles at the top. At her neck was a silver brooch with a heart held by a tiny cherub. Inga looked at the picture and saw her own eyes staring back at her.

"She's your grandmother," said Fru Pehrsdotter softly. Inga looked at the face in the picture again and knew what she would look like in ten years. "We were best friends for many years, and you look just like her."

Inga put the picture down and turned to Fru Pehrsdotter. She had a million questions to ask her, but another wagon had pulled up and a loud voice said, "You Hoo! Alma? Alma Pehrsdotter? There you are, come see all the milk we brought from Vasakull."

Fru Pehrsdotter disappeared out the back door to greet Inga's Aunt Mithilda Nilsdotter and her two daughters.

Inga's mouth went dry at the thought of spending the day with Aunt Mithilda. She didn't dislike her, it was just that Inga always felt insecure in her presence. Aunt Mithilda, her father's sister, was loud and overbearing. She liked to display her wealth in front of everyone. She wore expensive clothing and rings, and bragged about the cost of each thing she bought. She considered Sweden a backward country because of its folksy ways. She had married a wealthy farmer and businessman, Torvald Olsson, who took her to England and France several times a year, "to escape." She always had the most and the best of whatever she talked about. Mostly, she talked about herself or her two daughters, Amelia and Albertina. Aunt Mithilda brought milk for the *Ystmote*, but Inga knew she wouldn't participate in the making. She just wanted her share of the cheese and they had to tolerate her until she got it.

"Hello, Aunt Mithilda," Inga said meekly.

Her aunt, dressed in the latest French style, bustled past. Stopping half way down the hall, she looked back at Inga and said, "Why, hello, Inga." After eyeing Inga's clothes, she finally turned and continued down the hall.

Inga saw a farm boy deposit a container of milk from Vasakull on the grass.

"Tell Fru Nilsdotter I'll be back in an hour," said the boy.

"I will tell her," replied Inga as she watched him turn the wagon around and drive away.

"It's time to bring in more milk, Inga," said Hanna, handing Inga a pitcher. Together they began to make more trips to the kitchen. Inga could see that her aunt was the only adult not working. She was telling the women about her latest trip to the continent. Never had she known two girls, her cousins Albertina and Amelia, who were so totally useless at sixteen and eighteen years old. Neither of them had ever made a bed, baked a cookie, or washed their clothes. She only hoped they would marry rich men like their mother, so they could afford plenty of maids. Even though Åskeboda had farm hands and occasionally servants, the hired hands had always been treated like family, and Inga's family worked hard. Vasakull was said to go through maids like water; no one could stand the two girls or their mother ordering them around like slaves.

Even Inga's father, Ola, couldn't understand his sister or the man she married. There was always an element of competition between them. No matter how much Inga's father made, it never seemed enough to his sister, who looked at his home and family in disgust because they didn't travel or wear the latest fashions or send their children to boarding schools in Switzerland.

Inga didn't care. She liked her life and dreamed of being a farmer's wife. Thoughts of Henry Thorsell entered her mind. She tried to forget what had happened a month ago but could not. Even though she hadn't told a single person, she still felt it must have been her fault in some way. Why else would the boys try to attack her? Even Henry didn't look her in the eyes anymore. Did he think it was her fault too? A tear made its way down the front of her face to join the perspiration from the heat of the kitchen. She almost didn't hear Fru Pehrsdotter announce that the cheese-making was finished.

Bertha was helping several ladies put the cheese in the forms to cool and Hanna was washing the kettles they had used to boil the milk. Inga hurried to help Hanna get things ready to go back to the farm. It was almost 4 p.m. and the farm hands would soon be back to pick up the women. Inga asked her sister if she had ever seen the picture of their grandmother in the parlor.

Hanna said, "Yes, but I haven't thought of it in a long time."

"Do you think I look like Grandma Anna?" asked Inga.

"Why, yes, I guess you do," said Hanna. "I never thought of Grandma Anna as being young like us. I only remember her as being old in the picture in the parlor. She must have been forty-five or fifty then."

"Have you ever seen a silver brooch that looks like a cherub with a heart in *mor's* things?"

"Never, but maybe it was lost over the years."

Inga thought about the picture once again when Fru Pehrsdotter beckoned her into the parlor.

"I think you should have this picture," said Fru Pehrsdotter. "I'm getting on in years and have no little granddaughter to leave it to." She took the picture and gently laid it in a box for Inga. Inga thanked her graciously and smiled. Fru Pehrsdotter patted her shoulder and gave her a small hug before going back to the ladies in the kitchen.

Inga and the others rode silently back to the farm with Henry Thorsell again driving the wagon. Everyone was tired from standing on their feet all day, but for the rest of the year they would enjoy the delicious cheese that they had made. Inga leaned against her mother and dozed as the wagon continued down the lane between the birch trees. The late afternoon sun gave a red glow to the meadow as elk moved away from the trees to eat. Inga thought of the picture in the box and dreamed of the tiny fairy with the heart.

As the wagon pulled up to the farmhouse, Inga recognized her grandmother's beautiful dining room table, chairs, and sideboard sitting on a wagon by the front door. Bertha looked stricken dumb as she silently took in the meaning of it all. Suddenly, Inga's mother took action and as soon as Henry helped her off the wagon, she ran to find Ola.

"Oh, Ola, what are you doing with my mother's dining room set?" Bertha cried when she saw him.

Ola, stepping out of the front door with downcast eyes, quietly replied, "Don't worry Bertha, it's only temporary. I just need some quick cash."

Bertha searched for the real meaning in his face and then ran into the house and up the stairs, wiping her eyes with the corner of her soiled apron. She sat down on Michael's rocker as if the motion of it rocking would give her the answer she needed.

Inga turned to her father with questioning eyes. "Papa, tell me what has happened?"

Ola looked at his youngest daughter, then turned away. How could he explain to a child that he had lost at the horse races in Denmark and needed to pay off his debts? It was going to be tough enough explaining to Bertha. Ola walked into the front door and stopped before the stairs. He told himself he should go up and explain things to Bertha, but somehow he couldn't find the strength to do it. Instead, he turned toward the kitchen. Finding a bottle of *Akuavit* in the cupboard and ale in the cooler, he sat down at the long table and poured himself a small shot. Tossing the vodka down in a single gulp, he chased the burning sensation with the cool ale. The first swallow burned, but after that each one went down easier and easier and gradually the terrible shame he felt inside also began to ease.

Hanna and Inga fixed the farm hands their meal and Inga took a plate up to her mother, who was sitting motionless with her eyes closed.

"*Mor*, I made you some supper. Won't you eat? Please tell me why the furniture must leave," said Inga softly.

Bertha opened her eyes and motioned for Inga to lay the tray on the bed. "I'll eat later. Thank you Inga, dear. I can't tell you now. *Små grytor ha också öron*. Little pitchers have big ears." She noticed the housekeeper outside her bedroom. Then before Inga left she asked, "Inga, did your father eat anything?"

"No, *mor*, he only drinks tonight." Inga went back down to the kitchen to clean up after the farm hands and to help clear the dishes from the kitchen table.

"You go to bed, Inga, I'll finish the kitchen. You worked so hard today."

Inga was grateful to be out of the kitchen. She didn't like being around her father when he was drinking. It was only a matter of time before the fighting began. It was the same every time. Her father got drunk, her mother would go to her room to rock, and then her father would get angry and tell *mor* it was her fault he was losing money with the farm. Inga knew her mother would cry and Ola would leave the house in the early morning and they wouldn't see him for many days. When he returned, he always brought gifts and acted as though nothing had ever happened.

Inga's head swam with memories of other nights and other quarrels. She got into her nightshirt, climbed into bed, and pulled the curtains closed. She folded her hands tightly and said the children's prayer:

Gud som haver kär	God who loves the children
Se till mig some liten år	Watch over me, who is little
Vart jag mig i världen vänder	Wherever I go in the world
Står min lycka i Guds hånder.	My happiness is in God's hands
Lyckan kommer, luckan går	Happiness comes and happiness goes,
Den Gud älskar lyckan får	but he who loves God will have happiness always.

As she lay beneath the eiderdown quilts and crisp linen sheets, she suddenly thought of the dream that she had had about the man named Michael. As the month slipped by, she had forgotten his dire warning that the farm would someday be lost to the family. She remembered why the farm was called Åskeboda: five hundred years ago, the original Viking *långhus,* or long house, had been burned to the ground in a raid by the Germans. Would it happen again with this new house? It was only one hundred years old and fairly new compared to its neighbors.

It was hours later when Inga heard the dull footsteps of her father as he stumbled into his bedroom at the end of the hall. His gruff voice began to tear at Inga's soul as he shouted at her mother. Inga buried her head under the covers, plugged her ears with her fingers, and began to recite the Lord's Prayer so she wouldn't hear what was going on. Tears ran down her face and she felt helpless. For one fleeting moment, she wished her father would go away and never come back. But she was ashamed for even thinking such a terrible thought. She knew that she would always love him because, after all, he was her father.

CHAPTER 4
July 1889

Night is the time of the wanderers
When troll and gast use their power
To influence the fate of man.
And those who would be ponderers
Wait patiently for the magic hour
To ensure the devil's plan

*M*ichael looked at Inga through thick lenses that made his eyes appear smaller than they really were. His blond hair, stirred by the morning breeze, lifted from the top of his thinning crown as he walked toward her. At thirty, he was in the prime of his life. He had never been an outdoors type, but had spent his early years at the university studying agriculture and animal husbandry. His slender build belied the fact that he had built his farm into the most prosperous dairy in Blekinge through hard physical work and hours of bookkeeping.

Inga approached him cautiously, knowing that he was the love of her mother's life and the father of a half-brother that Inga barely remembered.

"Hello, Inga," said Michael in his deep resonant voice. "I'm glad *you know who I am now so I can speak to you. How is your mother?"*

"Hello, Michael," said Inga, not knowing if she should shake his hand and call him by his familiar name, something adults did when they greeted a friend. "My mother seems to be at peace now that I've told her about seeing you in my dreams."

"Good, I've worried about her since I've been gone. It seems like yesterday, though it's been twenty-five years." Michael took a deep breath and slowly let it out as he thought of how to tell Inga about the farm. "Your father is losing the farm, Inga. He never did know anything about farming when I knew him. Now things are bad. He's drinking and gambling more and I can see that my son will never get what he deserves. Your mother needs to prepare for the worst."

Inga thought of her father. He was a kind and loving man, but as the years had gone by, the children had had to supplement the family income in order to keep the farm prosperous, the boys by doing carpentry and Hanna by doing her weaving. Money had gotten tighter and tighter.

"Isn't there some way to keep Åskeboda?" It seemed inconceivable to Inga that she would have to leave the surroundings she loved.

"I'm afraid not. All of you must prepare for major changes," said Michael as he looked tenderly at Inga. "My time here is almost complete. I've waited only for you to reach out to me. Tell your mother I am always in her heart and I hear everything she says to me, and I will be waiting for her on the other side when it is her time." Inga didn't want the kindly man to leave.

"Michael, was my grandmother Anna really a witch?" asked Inga hesitantly, and Michael smiled at the question from the young girl.

"No, Inga. I didn't realize she had the sight when I first married your mother, but everything she told me came true. Even my death. She asked me not to go to France the last time, but she left the decision to me, and I went anyways. Your grandmother was the kind-

est, sweetest person I knew besides your mother, and we both have watched over you from the beginning, waiting for the second sight to appear. She will now guide you through your dreams to do what is right. She says her own grandmother did the same for her. Do not be afraid of the dead, but be careful of influences of evil, because negative forces will find you through your special gift." Michael turned and gave another look at the farm he loved, then slowly walked back toward the barn and disappeared into the bright moonlight.

Inga woke with a start as a cold breath of air crossed her cheeks and ruffled the curtains around the bed. She quickly pulled them aside and ran to the window, looking towards the barn where she had last seen Michael. In the moonlight, a shimmer of light wafted across the grass and then disappeared. Running downstairs and into the darkness outside, she realized that the sun was still below the horizon and twilight obscured most objects. As she peered into the shadows, it looked like large red eyes were staring back at her. Were they from an animal, or maybe a demon or troll? Years of frightening childhood stories came to mind and, unconsciously, she began to recite the Lord's Prayer. She could hear the call of the night birds and the cattle lowing in the barn as something disturbed their sleep, but the barn door remained closed tight. As she turned back to the house, she saw her mother staring out the upstairs window. She slowly retraced her steps up the stairs and back to her bedroom, wondering if her mother had the same dream.

Nestled back in her own bed, Inga found that sleep would not return. Instead, her thoughts went again and again to the words that both frightened and consoled her. She could still visualize Michael's face so clearly. Was he truly speaking to her from the dead? The hours dragged slowly by as she longed to tell her mother of her latest encounter with this gentle man. Inga could still feel the deep compassion and concern that he felt for his beloved Bertha.

CHAPTER 5
August 1889

August is ending; the hay is out to dry
The storehouse is empty and snowflakes soon will fly.
The pork barrel needs filling, the grain we must grind
Sausage we'll be making to hang from rafters high
September rains will come; the sun will soon depart,
We'll help each other gladly; we all must do our part.
But first we'll dance and laugh,
Drink ale and celebrate
We'll do the work tomorrow,
Then leave our souls to fate.

It was Saint Olof's Day, when all of Blekinge celebrated for the last time before the harvest. August was typically a slow month for the farmers, when vegetables and grain were reaching their peak before the cold rain and snow of winter. Everyone was going to the festival at the church except Inga's family, who were gathered around the table for breakfast with the hired hands.

Ola had told the family bad news the night before, and he was telling the farm hands this morning.

"This is just temporary," said Inga's father, "but I cannot guarantee being able to pay you next month, so you'll have to go. We're going to have to sell the cows and hay as soon as possible. At least you will have work. I found some harvesting at a farm north of here."

The farm hands looked at each other in disbelief. Some of them had been with the family for years. Inga glanced at Henry and then Hanna, who had tears streaming down her face. Ola's voice cracked as he spoke and Bertha stood up and walked up the back stairs to her bedroom. Soon, the family could hear the creaking of the floorboards as she began to rock back and forth in her favorite chair. The silence in the kitchen could be cut with the knives they were using to butter their bread. Hanna began to busy herself with the dishes as she looked out of the corner of her eye at Henry. Inga spoke up.

"Papa, they will be back after the harvest, won't they?"

"I don't know, I only know I must pay bills or we'll lose the farm by Christmas. In the spring, I'll buy a new herd and hire everyone back that still needs work."

Ola grabbed his light overcoat and walked forcefully out the door. The hired hands slowly got up from the table and headed out to their bunks, where they would pack up their few belongings. The last one to leave was Henry, who looked at Inga and then Hanna before going through the door. Only Inga remained standing at the table. Finally, looking at Hanna, she too began to clear the breakfast dishes and said, "Everyone is leaving, we can't have English lessons anymore, I have to quit school to help out on the farm, it's so unfair! What will we do now?"

"We must find extra work to help Papa save the farm," said Hanna.

Inga left the kitchen and walked through the parlor and formal dining room, which were now almost bare of furniture. Suddenly, an idea struck her.

"Hanna, with everyone leaving, let's close up part of the house. We'll live in only the kitchen and three bedrooms."

"Right! You are clever; with fewer rooms we'll use less heat. I'll move in the room next to yours and we'll get blankets to seal off the others. If we save every *öre,* we can have the farm back to normal by Christmas."

So Hanna and Inga never thought again of the festival. Instead, they began to work at saving Åskeboda. Hanna knew she would never see Henry Thorsell again unless they began to economize immediately. She would go to Ronneby and Malmö or even Stockholm to find extra work and on weekends she could still make linen.

Inga's mother rocked in her bedroom and talked to Michael. Her mind drifted in and out of reality as she began to see the end of her life. She had spent her whole life at Åskeboda and soon she may not be here at all. Where would she go?

She spoke to Michael softly, her lower lip quivering. "I know you will never forgive me if Ola loses the farm. It belongs to Karl and he must have it when he marries. Oh, Michael, I have made a mess of everything by marrying Ola!"

Inga walked into her parent's bedroom and listened to her mother talk. She threw her arms around her mother's neck and said, "Don't worry *mor*, Hanna and I will help with the farm. We'll have the farm hands back by Christmas and everything will be back to normal, you'll see." But she didn't let her mother see the fear in her eyes because she didn't believe a word she said. Instead, she hoped to get her mother's mind off her troubles.

"*Mor*, tell me again about Michael. What was he like? How did you meet?" Inga's mother began to tell her of the *Midsommerfest* thirty years before where Michael, a visiting agriculture student from the University of Stockholm, was introduced to her by her friends. How Bertha's mother knew immediately that Michael was the man her daughter would marry, and how their first child would be a boy. Inga smiled as her mother forgot the worries of the day and once again thought of happier times.

Meanwhile, Hanna was in the kitchen making a list of things to do to the house to save money. Soon, Inga joined her.

"*Mor's* taking a nap upstairs, what have you been writing since I've been gone?"

"It's a list of things we can do to save money. Here are my things: I will sell my linens and woolens I have saved for Christmas presents and the new dress I made for the holidays. Inga, you can start knitting sweaters, socks, mittens, and hats in the evening. You'll have to milk the cows and gather the eggs, then do the housework I usually do. I can work part-time in town until the roads become impassable."

"Good," said Inga, "I will ask to keep house for Fru Pehrsdotter after my work is done here. Do you think she will hire me?"

"I think so," noted Hanna as she wrote Inga's list on the paper next to hers. Hanna then looked around the kitchen at things they could sell in town. "How about selling some of the family's things, bed linens or household items we have made?" The list began to get larger as wooden baskets, towels, tablecloths, blankets, and other folk art was added.

Hanna finally got up from the table. "Let's start with the upstairs. The harder we work, the more we can think. Tomorrow, I will go to town with the hired hands and sell some items at the store. Hopefully Herr Stinson, the store owner, won't tell our neighbors where they came from and we will still have our pride."

Inga followed Hanna up the stairs to pull their best things from the cupboards to sell and move the furniture they need into one end of the house. By shutting off the fireplaces and hanging blankets from the doorways, only a few rooms on the kitchen end of the house would need to be heated in the coming winter. After finishing upstairs, they went downstairs to do the same, leaving the family only the kitchen, the porch, and the weaving room to heat. The heat from the kitchen would go up the back stairs and heat the bedrooms at night.

Hours later, when Bertha came down the stairs from her nap, she neither spoke nor acknowledged her daughters. Her mind had receded to a world of its own to keep the hurt of her life from destroying her. Although she walked and talked to her daughters and could still sit at her loom for hours, she was no longer capable of making decisions about her life. She neither saw nor heard Ola. She thought only of Michael and her mother, Anna, both of whom had been dead for over twenty-five years. She remembered only the dream she had where Michael told her that the farm was lost.

CHAPTER 6
September 1889

Rain falls on bare fields driving elk to the forest.
Frozen ground and cold nights leave outside work to the poorest.
Those who look to spring when summer has barely ended.
Know the rumbling of empty stomachs
Where the fear of death is fended.

Inga's feet touched the cold floor, sending a shiver up her back. It was her turn to start the fire in the kitchen before her mother awoke. She walked over to her old bowl and pitcher, which had been traded down from the beautiful china that once sat in her room, but the water in it was frozen. The window behind the heavy blanket that covered it was frozen with moisture, causing the ice to crack into beautiful art work she might have appreciated if she weren't so cold. Throwing a wool blanket around her shoulders and slipping heavy woolen stockings on her feet, she quietly walked down the cold hallway to the kitchen stairs, watching her breath steam in front of her face.

In the kitchen, she moved a few ashes from last night's fire in the huge wood stove to find the glowing embers. Seeing some, she sprinkled some wood shavings on the embers and grabbed the bellows hanging on the wall to give the embers a few good rushes of air to start them glowing. After placing more wood on the smoldering pile of ash, a bit of smoke began to find its way to the flue. Having started the wooden stove glowing, she then replaced the iron grate and moved a large pot to start boiling *gröt,* or oat gruel, for breakfast. In the butler's pantry was a sink and pump to get water. As she primed the pump, Inga thought of her day. She would do her chores in the house, starting with the milking, and then ride to Fru Pehrsdotters, then return home to finish the barn chores and collect the eggs.

As Inga was thinking, Hanna came down the stairs dressed and ready to milk the one lone cow in the barn. While she sat on the porch and put on the large men's boots, she spoke to Inga. "I will milk the cow this morning so you can get over to Fru Pehrsdotter's before the road unfreezes. It will be easier than walking the horse in the mud."

"What are you making for breakfast? The chickens have almost stopped laying." As Inga finished making the gruel and set it on the table, she said, "I'm only making *gröt,* we can save the eggs for Sunday. Tonight is Thursday, so we'll have pea soup with pancakes that will only use a little flour, milk, dried sausage and beans."

Hanna nodded and headed out to the barn that seemed large and lonely since the farm hands had gone and most of the cows had been sold. As the gruel and coffee began to boil, the warmth of the wood stove filtered up the stairs to heat the bedrooms. Only then did Inga go up to change her clothes. After a life of ease, it was very hard for Inga to come to terms with poverty. She no longer went into the empty rooms of the large house to dream of what used to be. Now she only hoped that her father had made enough money selling the household items and animals to make it to spring. Her mother had rarely talked the last month and her father rarely came home to see what his family was enduring. Inga no longer attended school and thoughts of college had faded into the past. She felt embarrassed to attend church when everyone in town had heard news of the family problems from Inga's Aunt Mithilda. And although many neighbors had offered help, Inga's family was too proud to accept any donations. Inga was tired of pea soup, chicken milk soup, and salt pork and gravy over rye bread, but the frugal meals were the staple of their existence now, along with smoked meats and sausages made the summer before. There was no variety in the food and no variety in day-to-day living during the dark fall months, as the sun stayed below the horizon more and more each day. Depression had settled over everyone in the family as gray wet days turned into sleet-filled nights.

Inga took breakfast up to her mother, then cleaned the kitchen and finished her morning chores; finally, she headed out the door to the barn where her horse was stabled. She would go to Fru Pehrsdotter's house to work four hours, then come back and clean the horse and cow stalls, gather the few eggs, do the second milking, and help Hanna with some weaving and carding. She no longer thought of *hustomten*. Her main concern was bringing a few *öre* into the house to keep her father from selling the farm. Fru Pehrsdotter had become a second mother to her now.

The air was unusually crisp and clear as she headed toward Fru Pehrsdotter's house on the horse with Peeka, her dog, following close behind. The rain had quit for a few hours, but everything was saturated with water and the half-frozen ground crunched as the horse walked along, finding more mud than road. It would not be long before the rain stopped and the snow began. Inga had seen migrant birds such as geese and swan heading south. The elk and snow hares had their winter coats and her horse would soon have its thick overcoat. All the small animals were sleeping in their dens and holes, and Inga's mother made sure the farm's *igelkott* had a nice warm place to have its babies. The cute little hedgehog, with its spines and long nose, lived in a small house that Inga's father made years ago and placed near the hedge where it was out of the way. The family was destitute, but hedgehogs always brought a little luck and the baby *igelkotts* were so cute to pick up and cuddle.

As Inga's horse neared the bridge at the Vierydsån, she paused to watch the small boats being readied for winter. Some were pulled near barns, turned over, and raised on boards where the barnacles could be removed and repairs made on the wooden sides. Others had already received bright new coats of white paint and were being stored in barns or boathouses. Activity along the river bustled as fisher wives took dried or smoked fish and placed them in barrels filled with salt to keep the fish edible all winter. Inga rode on to the large red house where they had made cheese earlier in the year. As she knocked quietly on the door of the back porch, she noticed a thin curl of smoke rising from the flue of the fireplace.

"Who is it?" asked a voice from the other side of the door.

"Just me, Fru Pehrsdotter, Inga." As the door opened, Inga stepped inside and removed her muddy boots, placing them on a rack near the fireplace. She hung her coat on a coat rack near the door and placed her handmade mittens and scarf over her coat, all the time speaking pleasantries to Fru Pehrsdotter.

"My, the mornings are getting colder," said the stooped old woman. "I don't know if my bones can take another winter."

"Sure they can," said Inga. "*Hej*, Herr Pehrsdotter," she said to Fru Pehrsdotter's son as he headed out the back door toward the cow barn with a wave to Inga.

"What would you like me to help you with today?"

"Why, I thought we'd go up to the attic and rearrange some of the boxes," said Fru Pehrsdotter.

The two women, young and old, walked up the stairs of the home that Inga was becoming familiar with. Although the house was not new, it was much more modern than Inga's. Many of the floors were covered with area rugs that Fru Pehrsdotter's husband had acquired on his travels to the Far East. Gas lights had been installed throughout the house, along with a gas heater and stove. They even had a toilet upstairs and down. Beautiful furniture, which was sent from around the world when the late Herr Petterson was in the military service, was found in every room. And the Petterson's had a library larger than the one in Bräkne-Hoby, with a ladder up to the higher levels. At church, the Petterson's sat in a coveted section that contained the family coat of arms on the wall over the pews.

"How old is Hjälmseryd farm?" inquired Inga as they began to straighten the attic.

"Well, this house is only thirty years old. It was built when my husband retired from the military. But the old house, the one near the street, is the original. At one time, the farmhouse and shed were completely enclosed in walls and had a large gateway entrance between the house and the barn. There were also smaller gateways near the pigsty and the woodshed. The whole yard was paved with cobblestones. The house was made of small logs with mud chinks to keep the family warm, while the other buildings were made of milled wood. Outside the house, there was a smaller building used to brew beer and spirits. All the roofs were turfed or thatched in the southern Swedish fashion, since most of Sweden's timber went to England during the Industrial Revolution in the early 1800s. The inside of the old house was just one room and a loft. The beds were built into the walls and had just a few cupboards, benches, and tables to fill the room. The fire was in the center and a flue took the smoke away from the inside. It was typical of an old farm after the Viking days were over. When I was a child, my father made all of the furniture, and my mother made all of our cloth on a loom in the corner. Of course, nowadays hardly anyone does that. That house is well over two hundred years old and even then, it is not the oldest around here. Some *långhus* are still in use even though they are falling apart. The poorest of the poor still live in them.

"Here, let us move this box over to that corner. When I was a small child, a Viking *långhus* stood on the ground where this house now stands. It was about six meters wide and twenty meters long. A room for the Lord and Lady of the manor was built in the back, and all visitors slept on benches around the sides. A fire was in the center of the main room and a hole in the roof let out the smoke. However, it must have been very smoky on the inside too. It could have been eight hundred years old, it was collapsing and the roof was falling in. During the Middle Ages, the house was used as a gathering place for Viking raiders. They had ceremonies in it and several families lived there. The Vikings actually hid their ships up the Vierydsån because the boats had a draft of only one meter even when they were fully loaded with horses, people, and food. And Vierydsån has easy access to the Baltic Sea at Vierydfjorden, the harbor down the river. The main village was nearer the ocean on the river, but it was difficult for marauders to find it because the houses were built close to the ground, their sod roofs hidden between the trees and bushes. Our country is rich with history even though it is poor for living."

"I've been to several people's houses that have Viking things in them. Things like rune stones and bowls and such. Why would people want those old things?" asked Inga.

"In France and the United States, I've read that they put old things in museums to keep them forever. Kind of a walking story so people don't have to read about history, but can walk through it instead. It's good for young people like you to know where they come from and why. France has old things from all over the world, from countries she has conquered. Someday, Sweden will have one for its old things."

"Is that why my mother keeps things that our family has had

forever? To show us the way things were? I guess it does make me appreciate what we have now."

"Yes, and some day you'll want to have those things to give to your children so they don't forget either. I'm sure your mother has a story to go with every old thing in your house, like I do with mine."

"You're right, I hear the stories every time we get them out. Every *Jul* I hear a story about the blue and white wall hanging that was in a Viking *långhus* on our property before our house was built."

"That's how we remember our past and keep those who died alive. Those who have gone before guide us and help us make good choices. Just as I know your Grandmother Anna watches over you."

As Inga looked around at all of the wonderful old things, she vowed to go up into her own attic and find her old dolls, furniture, and clothes stored there. Once again, she felt like a child of eight at *Jul* time.

Fru Pehrsdotter looked about and said, "Look around for an old black trunk, I have some things in it you might be interested in seeing."

Inga walked through the maze of furniture and lamps, pointing out trunks of various sizes and shapes until the one Fru Pehrsdotter was looking for was found. There it was, just small enough for Inga to carry. She heaved it up to an old table and fumbled with the pirate's lock in the dim light. Finally, the latch opened and Inga lifted the lid.

"There are a few things I think you should have in there."

"What things?" asked Inga as she tried to lift things out carefully while speeding up Fru Pehrsdotter's slow movements.

"Why, things from my childhood, and your Grandma Anna's too. Now slow down or you'll spill things."

Inga slowed down as much as she could, but anticipation got the best of her. She finally relented, letting Fru Pehrsdotter handle the things in the trunk while she looked on.

"See this box? It contains something very special," said Fru Pehrsdotter.

Inga took it in her hand and peeked into the tiny box. There, inside a piece of cloth, was the fairy holding the pink heart and a lock of hair.

"The fairy belonged to your Grandmother Anna, and the hair, too. When we were young, it was the fashion to make things out of hair and give it to your best friend: a watch fob, or a flower wreath. It is a tradition from Viking time. To have a piece of someone is to make you 'sisters,' to hold that person dear to your heart. It's why we keep the old things from our past. That's why we have attics, I guess, to keep the memories and people alive."

Inga placed the little fairy in her hand and felt a warm glow go up her arm and settle into her stomach. She barely heard what Fru Pehrsdotter said when she handed her some old letters, an embroidered piece of linen, and some old daguerreotypes. For Inga, the fairy was what connected her to the grandmother she never knew. She looked at the brooch for several minutes and then tucked it and the other items back into the small box for later. Fru Pehrsdotter and Inga worked on organizing the attic for another two hours before she said goodbye and went back to her own farm. She put the small box of items in her tall wooden bed so she could see them every night before she went to sleep.

CHAPTER 7
October 1889

I looked into the eyes of death
And knew the meaninglessness of life.
Nothing lay beyond the boundaries
Of our earthly strife.

Men will not be judged
By their virtues or their deeds
But by whom they undermine
And how they succeed.

The Devil is the savior of
Those who do ill.
Join him at the judgment seat
Thy coffers to fill.

Inga stirred in her bed as the dream settled into her subconscious. Moaning escaped her lips as she tried to avoid what was seizing her mind. Her breathing became rapid and sweat broke out on her forehead. Soon, her arms flailed around her as if they could stop her mind from slipping into the hole where bad dreams occur. This dream was different, it wasn't going to be pleasant, and it wasn't going to remind her of the old days.

As a breeze filtered through an open window and into her enclosed bed, Inga stirred. She was just about to sleep when she heard the bumping noise on the stairway, like a box being lifted step by step. As a foot treaded on the landing, a familiar creak told her that the second board had been reached. Inga peeked out of her curtain and noticed her door stood ajar.

The noise became a scraping sound, as if something heavy was being dragged down the hallway to her room. She quickly got up and ran across the cold floor to lock the door, then she sat with her back against the cold wood. The noise continued: scrape, stop, scrape, stop, until it paused behind the door. She braced herself against it to keep whatever was on the other side out, but the door began to move against the old lock, slightly at first and then more and more until the wood was straining from the push.

Inga looked at her reflection in the mirror above her washbasin and saw the outline of a face and two hands pushing on the door as if it were a thin sheet. Inga ran back to her bed, jumped onto the quilt, and shut the curtains. The clawing hands began to bang on the door, first softly and then faster and harder until the pounding vibrated all around the room. Inga put her hands to her ears, but the noise was like artillery being fired from a castle wall. When Inga thought she might go deaf, the noise stopped and left her in silence, which was even more disturbing. Did they leave? Who were they? Softly, an apparition appeared beside her, glowing and moving like a petticoat blown in a summer breeze. Inga shivered, but it somehow gave her the comfort she needed. Who was this gast*? Why was it here?*

She peeked through the curtains across the room and saw the doorknob turn and the door slowly open. There stood six cloaked figures with black hoods and priestly robes. At their fronts were long, beaded necklaces from which hung distorted golden crosses. Across their backs were thick ropes attached to a wooden coffin. Inga watched as the six figures strained and pulled the coffin across the floor. As it drew near, she peered through the glass lid that showed her father staring wide-eyed at her. His face was locked into a grotesque scream and his fingers had frozen while scratching the lid to get out. Inga shivered as the coffin was slowly dragged in front of her bed and out through the door that connected her room to Hanna's.

Inga woke up shivering and quickly shut the curtains. In the darkness, she saw the *spåke* next to her and felt a small hand grasp her own. She fell asleep comforted as the apparition of her grandmother began to sing.

> *"Goodnight, my angel, it's time to close your eyes.*
> *I will watch over you as I sing a lullaby.*
> *I will never leave you, I always will be near.*
> *So sleep my little angel, there is no need to fear..."*

Inga woke with a start, her bedclothes drenched with perspiration as she shivered in the night. She looked down at her hand and saw it was curled like it was holding an object; she let out a scream and dropped whatever it might have held. Within a few seconds, Hanna had found her way into the bedroom. Without asking what troubled her, Hanna wrapped her arms around her sister and they held each other close until they fell asleep together.

CHAPTER 8
November 1889

*The sun begins to disappear
and Swedes grow melancholy.
Sadness is dragged into every home
with dreams of fools and folly.
Fear sits in a farmer's mind,
knowing of his race with time,
the food may not last 'til spring,
thus death and dying may it bring.*

Inga quickly opened the door as Hanna brought a load of wood from the woodshed. The rain was coming down in sheets, as if the sky had opened up a dam. Hanna's boots were covered with thick mud past the ankles.

"Where has the snow gone?" Hanna asked.

"I don't know, it seems to rain longer and longer every year. The yard looks like a lake all the way to the barn," replied Inga. "I'm tired of the rain. The house stays dark, everything is damp, and no one comes to visit in weather like this," sighed Inga to Hanna. "I'm afraid it will be at least a month before its cold enough to freeze the mud again so the horses can walk on the road."

Inga smiled. She knew her sister would be thinking about Henry Thorsell, who had stopped by several times in the last month to ask if the family needed anything. Henry was working as a carpenter's helper in Ronneby, three miles from Åskeboda. The road would be impassable for wagons and carriages until the ground froze. Hanna loaded the wood into the fire box and walked dejectedly to the weaving room, where she worked on some linen for the store in Malmö. Inga took a fresh baked loaf of rye bread out of the oven and began to whistle a sad song.

"What is that song you're whistling?" inquired her mother as she walked down the back stairs.

"I don't know, something I heard once."

"It's the tune to a lullaby my mother used to sing to me when I was a small child," said her mother. "I haven't heard anyone sing it in years."

"How do the words go?" asked Hanna from the weaving room.

"Let's see, something about

"Goodnight, my angel, it's time to close your eyes.
I will watch over you as I sing a lullaby.
I will never leave you...."

"Oh, I can't remember the words," replied her *mor*.

Inga felt a shudder go up her spine as a piece of the nightmare came back to her. Her father's coffin, the look of horror on his face, the scraping of wood on her floor upstairs; in a trance, she began to rock back and forth, singing the words to the lullaby the apparition had sung to her.

"That's it, that's the song my mother used to sing. Where did you hear it?"

Inga looked at her mother. Should she tell her about the dream, or let fate take its course? She knew it was only a matter of time before her father died.

"I, I don't remember," stuttered Inga.

Inga's father came in the door, unshaven and smelling of alcohol. He played with the logs in the wood stove and then took his place in the chair at the end of the kitchen table without saying a word to the family. Peeka got up from his spot in front of the stove to lie down next to his master.

"I've got a man coming out to look at the farm in a couple days," he finally said.

"Why would a man come to see the farm now?" Inga replied, suddenly interested in the conversation. "It's closed up, most of the furniture is gone and the weather is intolerable."

Bertha spoke to her husband for the first time in a month. "Why would anyone be interested in my son Karl's farm?"

"It's time to sell it. We will lose everything if we wait much longer."

"What are you talking about? It's not yours to sell, it belongs to Karl."

"I'm talking about me, selling the farm, to pay off my gambling debts," confessed Ola. "We'll move into a place in Ronneby until our finances get better, then we'll buy another farm,"

"Have you gone mad? Do you think I will let you sell the farm that has been in my family for over two hundred years?" shouted Bertha.

"You don't have a choice. When you married me, the farm became mine, and the bank will take it for taxes if we don't sell it soon. At least this way, we will get enough for a small house, a garden, and our furniture after my debts are paid," announced Ola, not caring that the girls would know the truth.

"What do you mean 'our furniture?' Everything in this house was here when I married you: the land, the animals, the furniture, everything. You brought nothing to this marriage and that is the way you will leave it. You can go to the poor house, but I will not. The children and I will go to live with my sister, and I will take what's mine with me!"

"You can't be serious. I've worked twenty-five years on this place. It is mine by law, women don't own anything," taunted Ola.

"You. I cannot stand to look at you. You have lost everything my Michael built. The farm has gone downhill since the day you arrived. I want you out tomorrow."

"You cannot mean that, Bertha. We have been married twenty-five years. You cannot be so heartless. You will change your mind."

"Change my mind? I will pack your things now before I do."

Inga watched as her mother climbed the stairs to the bedrooms. She could hear footsteps walking above as her mother climbed the attic stairs in search of a trunk for her father's things. Inga's father stood up and went to the cupboard where the vodka was stored.

Inga went into the weaving room to discuss with Hanna the conversation between her mother and father. Fear began to well up in her chest as the talk of the day replayed in her mind.

Upstairs, Bertha finally found a trunk that would hold Ola's things. Inside were old clothes which had been stored since her mother had died years ago. Bertha thought to herself, "What have I done? I am over fifty years old and soon will have no farm and no husband." Women in Sweden rarely divorced and stayed in marriages without love forever. If only Michael was still alive, this would never have happened. The longer she knew Michael, the more she loved him, and in the five years they were married, she felt she couldn't love anyone more. When their son Karl was conceived, he waited on her hand and foot until labor came. He cried like a baby with joy when she delivered and both were healthy. It was only a few weeks after that the boat he was on sank off the coast of Denmark. Then, when her parents died, her *mor* of influenza and her *far* of a broken heart, she thought her world had ended.

Bertha had met Ola before Michael's death. Ola was the local constable and he and some friends had come to Åskeboda to see the farm and ask Michael questions about the operation of the farm, but Michael was always cautious about answering them. He didn't know why, he just felt that the men weren't completely honest in their intentions. When Michael died, Ola had been one of the first to offer his condolences to Bertha. He had sent her flowers regularly with sweet messages of encouragement. Finally, he showed up at the farm and proposed to her. She was taken aback by his sudden question, but she and little Karl had been so lonely and she was anxious about the farm. She had looked over Michael's books and couldn't understand them.

Ola was dark and handsome and closer to her age, being twenty-five. He played with little Karl and said he wished he had a fine son like him, bringing Karl toys from Europe. They had married a few months later and one day, while Bertha was visiting friends, Ola packed up all of Michael's possessions, pictures, and momentos into a trunk and put them into the attic. Only his rocking chair and his records of Åskeboda remained of her life with Michael.

Bertha's hands quickly placed Ola's clothes from the bed into the old trunk and she started dragging it down the stairs. She remembered the last twenty-five years. The big farm had slowly been going downhill as the money was tighter and tighter. Five children had been born, Inga, the last, when she was thirty-nine years old. The pregnancy and childbirth had left her in a weakened condition, but today she felt as young as she did the day they were married. Today was the last time Bertha wanted to set her eyes on Ola.

At 10 p.m. the girls had gone to bed, but Ola was still in the kitchen, having never moved from the chair except to relieve himself occasionally. The bottle of *Aquavit* was finished, and Peeka deserted him for the blanket on the back porch.

Speaking gruffly to himself, he said, "By the devil, this house is mine and I'll do with it as I want. No woman is going to tell me how to run my farm."

Slowly, his eyes lifted to a flickering shadow in the corner. Was it a troll? Ola got up from the table and took a gun off the shelf. Fumbling with the gun and nearly falling off the bench, he loaded it with several bullets. Crawling on the floor on his hands and knees, he looked behind the furniture to see if anything was hiding in the shadows. Peeka began to whine as his master dragged the gun along the floor, stumbling and weaving as he walked.

Pulling himself to his feet, Ola opened the back door and looked out into the dark night, searching for the trolls that were invading his home. A full moon was showing through the rain clouds that passed overhead and the wet yard shimmered like a lake. Putting the gun in his pants, he grabbed a loaf of bread, some meat from the cooler, and a hymnal, and walked out into the dark and windy night to perform an ancient ritual to foretell the future. Standing with his face turned to the moon, he made a wish, bowed three times, and opened the book to read his fortune. The first line that caught his eye said, "*Vad som göms i snö kommer upp it tö.*" What is hidden in snow comes forth in the thaw. A terrible omen, Ola felt his secret gambling would soon be told to everyone in town, and the farm would be lost forever.

"Curse you trolls and curse you moon, for sending me a spell." Wide-eyed and out of his mind from his drinking, Ola dropped the bread and meat and began ripping the pages from the book in an attempt to remove the words from his mind. As he looked up, he saw several trolls peeking from the side of the house, from behind the tree, and from the shed. Ola ran to the barn with Peeka in pursuit. Closing the barn door behind him, he turned to see the little demons advancing upon him. He rummaged through tools and implements until he turned up a hayfork and sat on a three legged milking stool. The barn door slowly swung open and the moon's rays hit his face and begin to affect his mind. Ola's bleary eyes saw the trolls, who had come to capture his mind with their evil power. He vaguely remembered the words to the Lord's Prayer, but soon mixed them up in his attempt to banish the trolls. Pulling the gun from his pocket, he tried to focus his eyes on them but all he could see was the saliva dripping from their teeth as they came closer and closer.

As the trolls got to Ola, they began to pull on his clothing, take off his shoes, and tear at his hair. Ola pointed the gun at one and then another, trying to scare them away, but to no avail. He retreated to a corner of the barn, crawling, while the trolls began whispering and laughing at his desperate attempts to escape them. One large troll turned the large gun in Ola's hand and, holding the barrel to Ola's temple, pulled the trigger.

At 10:27 pm, as the family slept, the trolls dragged Ola's spirit, captured in a wooden box, to *bergakungen*, the hall of the mountain king.

The family awakened as Peeka howled a mournful song to the spirits of the night. Inga, Hanna, and their *mor* ran to the windows to try to understand why the dog was howling, but all that they could see were the red eyes of something in the dark and a flash of teeth with a hideous smile.

CHAPTER 9
December 1889

Good King Wenceslas looked out
On the feast of Steven
When the snow laid round-a-bout
Deep and crisp and even.
Brightly shone the moon that night,
Though the frost was cruel,
When a poor man came in sight,
Gath-ring winter fuel.

Traditional Folk Song

It was almost Christmas Eve in Inga's household, but there was no Christmas tree decorated in the foyer, no aspen leaves surrounding the door, no holly sprigs or decorations in the home. The house was in mourning and Ola's body was still in the barn, even though it had been a month. The ground had been too frozen to dig a grave, and the road was too soft from the rain to take the wagon into Bräkne-Hoby for a funeral. Inga's mother had taken charge of the funeral arrangements, and with a break in the weather she hoped to have a boat waiting at the Vierydsån. The boat would take the coffin around the southern end of the river at Vierydfjorden and on to Bräkne-Hoby Lutheran churchyard to be buried. Henry Thordson was working in the barn, making a wooden coffin for Ola's body. He had volunteered to do this because of his respect for the family. Close neighbors braved the rain and mud to send over covered dishes to the family. *Husmanskost*, or yellow pea soup with salt pork and onions, salt herring and sour cream, pork sausages and pickled beets, baked brown beans with bacon, and fruit soup. There was also *pitepalt*, potato dumplings stuffed with pork, *spettekaka* the towering egg and sugar cake almost a yard high that took six or seven dozen eggs to make, and cheesecake that was more like a pudding and accompanied by cherry compote, which rivaled the sweetness of the towering cake. Eels on their migration to the sea had been caught and smoked for the family and *Jansson's Temptation,* or potatoes with anchovies, cream, and onions were in the kitchen for the few visitors that braved the mud.

Finally, just before *Jul*, the weather had turned cold and the ground had frozen solid. Henry brought the wagon and horse around with Ola in the wooden coffin in the back and the whole family and their friends walked Ola to the Vierydsån, where a boat was to meet them. It had been arranged for the boat to take the coffin and Bertha around to the harbor near Bräkne-Hoby, where a wagon would take the body to a service planned at the church. The rest of the family and the neighbors would ride in wagons to the service. After unloading the wooden coffin, Henry turned the wagon toward the road and stopped to let the others ride in the back.

Henry helped Inga into the wagon first, making sure she had enough blankets to keep her warm. "Are you warm enough?" asked Henry in his lilting Swedish. Inga was surprised that he was talking to her.

"Yes, I will be fine," she answered. "Thank you for making the coffin for father."

"It is the least I could do after all the years I worked here," said

Henry. "Hanna, where are you going to live after the house is sold?"

Hanna replied, "I am moving to Stockholm to work in a factory there; the wages are low but higher than I can make here. I'll find a roommate in a boarding house for women and study for a nursing license, then maybe go to Canada to live with my brothers and their wives."

Henry's lips tighten to a straight line. "Will you give me an address so I can visit you if I ever get to Stockholm?"

"Certainly. I haven't got a place yet, but I'll send the address to my mother when I get it," Hanna replied as she looked down at her feet. The thought of never seeing Henry again caused her eyes to water. "Stockholm is 400 kilometers away, why would you go there?"

"To see you," said Henry softly, his face turning red from embarrassment.

Henry turned then and helped Inga and Fru Pehrsdotter into the back of the wagon, then went to the front to climb aboard next to Fru Pehrsdotter's son. The wagon was the first of a line of five wagons going to the church for the funeral service. Slowly, the horses and wagons went down the road as the wheels got stuck in ruts in the frozen ground. As they drove the long road, neighbors came out and waved or stood by somberly as the procession went by. Everyone knew Ola Nilsson.

The trolls in the wood behind large rocks and trees giggled with glee at the sight of the coffin in the wagon. The *hustomten* sighed as their family rode away. Who would take care of them now? What would happen to the farm? Inga also wondered what would happen to their family when everyone was living in separate places. Her family was the only thing she cared about, and it was falling into pieces. She remembered that only a year ago she was a happy fourteen-year-old living the dream. They had had a lovely farm, friends and neighbors who loved her, a family who was together every night in a beautiful house. Her favorite horse, her loving dog and cat, even the cows were her pets, each having a name and stall of their own. Yes, it was hard work to keep the farm going, but where would she go? Everything was to be sold and auctioned off. Nothing would be left of her life. Tears came to her eyes as she remembered the life she had known. No parents, her sister gone, Henry gone. She felt as if she were all alone in the world.

CHAPTER 10
January 1890

Where are the blessings that I deserve?
Where is the God that watches over?
Is there a being that holds the earth?
Why does He hide from me?
If He can guide the wind and stars
If He can watch the whale and plover
Why can't He control my life?
Am I not good enough for Thee?

The snow was turning to slush and everything below it was brown and ugly. There was not a hint of spring in the air, but on this day the farm called Åskeboda was sold to the highest bidder, and that was Uncle Torvald, her father's brother. Inga wondered what was to become of her. Her mother had arranged to be moved into the home of her sister. Bertha would share a room with two of her sister's daughters, but at least she had a bed. Inga stood outside her home and watched as the last of the furniture was loaded onto a neighbor's wagon to be driven away. Hanna had already moved to Stockholm and gotten a job in a factory, and Inga had her new address in her pocket. Her small satchel of clothes was at her feet. Soon, a large surrey appeared on the road. It was her

Aunt Mithilda and her two daughters, Amelia and Albertina, with their father Torvald. As they drew nearer, Inga got a sick feeling in the pit of her stomach.

"Hey, Inga, we're here to take you and Bertha to your new homes," said Mithilda. Both girls tittered and buried their faces in their warm winter muffs. They were dressed in warm leather coats with sheep's wool lining. Their hoods were also sheep's wool with a trim of fox around the edges, matching the muffs they carried.

"Inga," said her mother, "I've arranged for you to live with Aunt Mithilda."

Inga looked at her mother like she had lost her mind. "Aunt Mithilda? I don't want to live with them. I don't even like them."

"Inga!" said her mother, looking embarrassed. "They have asked if you can stay with them, and I consented. You will be taken care of there."

"Yes," said her aunt. "You will get everything that my daughters get, you will be treated like my own child, and we would love to have you!" The daughters giggled into their muffs again, not looking at Inga at all. Inga looked straight ahead as the surrey turned and headed to Bräkne-Hoby. Vasakull, their large home, was on the north side of town. When they reached Bräkne-Hoby the surrey stopped at Bertha's sister's house, where several children and grandchildren welcomed them. The brown house was small but neat. Inga's Uncle Karl, Bertha's brother-in-law, was a shopkeeper and his children helped him run the store. Bertha was to help with the smaller children and the housework, something she had not done in many years, but it was a place for her to stay until the tax on the farm was paid and she would receive the leftover money from the sale.

"It's only until we get some money, then we will find a place together so you can finish school and start college at the *Folkhögskolen*. We will be together soon, Inga." Bertha showed with her eyes that Inga was not to make a scene in front of the relatives.

"All right, *mor*," said Inga resolutely. "I'll stay with Aunt Mithilda." When Inga's *mor* was settled in her new home and her things put away, Inga and her aunt's family got back into the surrey and headed for their home.

"You'll see your mother at church on Sundays, Inga. You'll be fine," said Mathilda. Inga doubted that things would be "fine," and her face looked like a thunder storm was about to let loose with tears, but she continued on in silence and looked at her feet for the rest of the ride to Vasakull.

The surrey stopped in front of the home, which was much bigger and much fancier than the farm. There was a long double porch on the front of the house, painted green with white trim. The house stood on a small hill, so the rest of the homes nearby were below it. The yard was beautiful even in the winter; bushes and trees were planted and trimmed along the walk up to the stairs and the wide porch. Inga looked up at the second-floor porch where two servants were looking down at their new charge. Their faces were stern and unhappy at the sight of the family. The house was close to some neighbors, not on a farm like Inga's house. Aunt Mithilda and Uncle Torvald's farm was near their home, but not close enough to be seen. Their animals, barn, and farm hands were not in sight. Inga knew immediately that she would not be happy in this home. She missed her horse, her dog, and her cat, which had stayed with her old home and the new farm hands that would take care of it.

"We won't be going back to Åskeboda," said her aunt. "I've told the farm hands to board up the doors and windows since we won't be using it. The new farm hands will be living in the barn and preparing their own food, just like the farm hands on our farm."

Inga grabbed her small suitcase and got down from the surrey with no help from her uncle. While she walked up to the front door with her aunt and cousins, Torvald took the surrey to the back of the main house where the carriage house stood; a servant boy was there to take the surrey from him. There were four horse stalls and a place for the surrey to park, but it was too small for cows, pigs, or chickens. They were all at the farm on the north end of town.

"Come up to the second floor," said Aunt Mathilda as she removed her coat and muff, handing them to a waiting servant. Her daughters did the same and they continued up the stairs. "I'll show you where you are to sleep and keep your things."

Inga followed the girls up the stairs and peeked in each room as they passed. All the bedrooms were large and beautiful. Real silk wallpaper, not stencils, looked stunning on the walls. The master bedroom had a huge four-poster bed of black wood with thin white drapes hung around it. The fireplace was burning even during the day, and a settee and chairs faced the marble front. A small chest with a large gas chandelier hung from the center of the room and a desk stood in front of a bay window. Beneath the furniture was a beautiful Persian rug made to the size of the room.

In the girls' rooms, each had a smaller four-poster bed with the same sheer drapes around them. Amelia's room was done in pink, while Albertina's room was a soft pale green. The floor was covered in thick wool rugs that matched the silk bed covers in matching colors. Although the rooms were slightly smaller than the master, they also had a desk and shelves, and fainting couches in front of fireplaces, which were lit. The windows were covered with silk drapes and heavy wool drapes that were pulled to the side in the daytime to let the sun shine in. Small dressing rooms were attached to each bedroom with large wardrobes to hold dresses and shoes. Inga took a breath at the sight of each room. Each was more beautiful than the last. But Inga wondered about the water closet, and where would they do ablutions? There were no China pitchers or wash basins in the rooms.

A room at the end of the long hall was small and undecorated. It contained a small woodstove with an iron on top, a dry sink and a pitcher, a small, plain bed, and hooks for clothing on the wall. A peddle sewing machine stood near the window. On the opposite side of the hall was a bathroom with a working toilet, a long narrow bath tub, and a sink, something Inga had never seen in any home in Bräkne-Hoby.

"The small room will be yours, Inga. The bathroom is for my daughters. You will use the bathroom outside the back door along with the servants. I will give you a list of chores that you will do every day and every week. With you here, we can get rid of one of the servants, since you will need to earn your keep if you want any clothes. I think Albertina's will fit you when she finishes with them." Aunt Mithilda narrowed her eyes at Inga, turned on her heel, and left Inga standing in the middle of the small room. Inga stood with her mouth open. What was going on? What would happen to her? She sat on the small bed and looked at the iron and sewing machine. "I guess I am their new upstairs maid," she said to herself. "Wait until I talk to my mother."

The kitchen bell rang and everyone was expected at dinner. Inga changed into her best clothes and walked down the stairs to the formal dining room where family was to eat. Aunt Mithilda looked at Inga and motioned her to the kitchen. "You will eat with the other servants and help in the kitchen whenever we have guests." Inga looked at her clothes and saw that her cousins were wearing beautiful dresses, while Inga was dressed in her best farm clothes. Inga got up from her chair and walked into the kitchen to acquaint herself with the servants and took a seat at the long wooden table with trestle benches. The servants, Gunilla and Karin, gave Inga a glance out of the side of their eyes and kept talking low to each other. The stable hand and the driver introduced each other, while the two cooks waited for Inga to introduce herself.

"Hello," said Inga. "I am a cousin of the family and have just come to live here."

All of the servants turned to look at Inga and shook their heads. The cook whispered, "I feel sorry for anyone working in this house. You will learn the punishments soon enough." Inga shivered at the warning, the hairs rising at the base of her neck.

After dinner, Inga was in her room hanging up the few clothes that she owned when Albertina and Amelia dropped off several pieces of clothing to be mended. "Inga, I hope you can sew, these things need mending and we like our clothes washed and ironed after each use." Inga nodded and looked at the cousins with squinted eyes.

"I will have to learn to iron. We had servants to do that at our house," she replied.

"I'm sure you will learn soon enough," said Amelia. "The other servants can show you how it's done."

As Inga pulled down her bedclothes to sleep, her aunt came into the room and gave her a list of chores. At the top of the long list was gathering wood for the fireplaces, weeding the garden, washing, drying and ironing the family clothes, mending anything that needed mending, helping in the kitchen when needed, and shining the shoes worn by the family. Inga could not believe all that she would have to do. When would she go to school? When would she have any time for herself? Her heart broke at that moment, knowing that she would never have a normal life again. Living in this beautiful house would be like a prison sentence with hard labor.

As her aunt left the room, her Uncle Torvald stuck his head in past the door. "Inga," he said, as he looked her up and down with glinting eyes, "I hope you like it here. We will do everything we can to make your life enjoyable." He smiled and winked his eye. Again, Inga's neck began to tingle. What was her uncle talking about? Why did he look at her so? Inga closed the door and locked it, then began undressing and hanging her clothes on a hook. She snuggled down into the wool blanket and sheets and said her prayer to God.

"Dear God in Heaven. Why am I here? Why will I suffer the indignities of becoming a servant when I have always treated everyone with respect? Help me to understand...Our father who art in heaven, hallowed be thy name..."

When Inga got up in the morning, servants were already moving about the house. She quickly dressed, ran down the stairs, and asked where the wood was stacked. She would fill the baskets near the downstairs fireplaces first, then those found upstairs while the family was eating breakfast. She looked out to the garden behind the house and noted that someone had hoed rows of dirt, but no seeds were planted yet. Inga went into the kitchen to hurriedly eat breakfast before going upstairs to bring down the washing. Already she was tired. The cook pointed to a large kettle that stood in the backyard above a fire pit, so Inga again went to the woodpile to get some fire started under the kettle. She went to a pump where a bucket stood and began pumping the water out of the well until her arms ached. It took five buckets of water to fill the kettle halfway. Taking a knife and shaving some soap into the kettle, she then stirred the water with a large smooth stick until she could see suds at the top of the water. She ran back up the stairs and retrieved the clothing that was meant to be washed that day. Dumping the clothes in the kettle, she took the stick and stirred the water. When the clothes had been stirred for ten minutes, she laid them on a piece of linen and began emptying the kettle water into the garden and then refilled the bucket again to rinse the clothes. Her small hands were too little to wring the clothes when they were rinsed, so she laid them again on the linen until the water had drained out of them, then carried each piece of clothing to a rope and hung them on the line halfway so they would not drop off in the wind. She emptied the water in the kettle using the bucket and dumped the water into the garden. When it rained, she would hang the clothes in the basement.

By this time it was lunch, and the family was up and eating, so Inga ran back to the woodpile and brought in wood for the baskets in the bedrooms. After making three trips, she sat down for her lunch in the kitchen, potato soup with leeks and bacon fat served with large chunks of fresh bread. Inga was so hungry she ate every bite, but when she asked for seconds she was told the servants only got one portion each. Inga put her dishes in the large farm sink and ran up the stairs to see what needed to be sewed and ironed. She then noticed the iron on the small potbellied stove and again ran down the stairs to get wood to fill the stove. As she came back to her room and tried to fill the stove, she noticed the wood was too large to fit in it. She took the wood back down the stairs and into the backyard and found a small axe, which she used to splinter the wood into smaller pieces. Once again, she brought the wood up to her room and tried again to get the stove to light. Needing paper, she ran down to the cook and asked for matches and newspaper, which had been read by the family a week prior. Finally, returning to her room, she got a small fire in the stove started and waited for the iron to warm. Looking around the room, she found a wooden board with legs leaning against the wall which she could use to iron the dresses and shirts the family had worn that had been previously washed. Never having ironed before, by the end of the day Inga was exhausted and covered with burn marks on her hands from handling the heavy, hot metal iron. She had only burned one shirt lightly and hoped that it would not be noticed. She then heard the dinner bell, changed her clothes and, exhausted, walked down the stairs to the kitchen to eat. Inga sat with the other servants and, as they talked about their day, she slowly closed her eyes and fell asleep with her head on her hands until someone nudged her and told her dinner was done and to finish her chores. Inga went outside to get the laundry that had dried, then slowly walked up the stairs just as her aunt was going by. Aunt Mathilda looked at her tired niece and said, "Now that you know your chores, I expect them to be done twice as fast. The garden will need weeding and planting within the month and the stable boy will help you hoe the rows until it's finished. Then he will go back to his chores." Inga nodded and returned to her room where the mending was waiting. Sitting on her bed, she picked the first piece to be mended when her aunt returned.

"I found this shirt with a burn on the sleeve. You will have to rewash it and lay it in the sun to bleach the stain out of it. It had better not happen again, or I will take the switch to your legs."

"I'm sorry," said Inga, "I've never ironed before and find it difficult to keep the iron hot and then keep it moving, it is very heavy."

"I will accept no excuses," said her aunt as she turned to walk away.

Inga was so tired, she put her mending aside and crawled into bed in her clothes. Her room was hot because of the stove, and the small window did not give much ventilation. She had been asleep about an hour when her uncle came into the room quietly, kissed her head, and gave her blankets a pat. Inga's eyes were open in a flash. Why was he in her room? He left immediately and she closed her eyes and slept until morning.

The following day went a lot smoother because Inga knew where everything was and what was to be done. She hoped the weather cooperated. Even though it was winter and cold, the sun was shining and the wash and garden could still be tended as long as there was no snow. Winter vegetables could be planted and buried under straw to keep them from freezing. She knew that when it stormed or froze the laundry would be impossible to do outside. She was told that during bad weather, she would be doing the laundry in the dark, cold basement where a kettle also sat. Inga would be heating water on the cook's stove and walking down a flight of stairs into the dark with the hot water bucket. Oil lamps would be her only light and the clothes would be hung across a rope strung from wall to wall. She did not look forward to that. Because the garden was still not frozen, just cold and slushy, she went up to her room to do the mending earlier in the day and marveled at the lovely clothes her cousin wore. They were from France and in the latest fashions. Inga wore her farm clothes every day. She only had three changes: two for week days and one for Sundays when she got to see her mother. But even on Sundays she did not see her mother for long. The preferred church pew where her family had sat as one of the wealthiest families in town was now occupied by Inga's Aunt Mathilda and her family. Inga would be relegated to the servants' pews in the back. The winter was hard on her *mor's* health. Her fingers would stiffen, her back would ache, and she needed a cane to walk from her sister's house in town to the church. Inga did not see her often, and when she was there, Aunt Mathilda would make sure she only got a hug and a few words with her mother. She never had time to tell her of her living conditions, the work she was required to do, or the weirdness of Uncle Torvald at night.

CHAPTER 11
May 1891

Life has changed and darkness fills the earth
I live in a box with no doors or windows
Where is the life I had growing up?
Where are the people I loved so much?
What will happen to me?
I see only hopelessness.
I see only sorrow.

Inga, her sister Hanna, and Henry Thorsell were standing in front of the barn at Åskeboda looking at the house that was boarded up and dilapidated. As they stood watching, the house began to fall into itself, the roof collapsing and the windows breaking as a long groan came from it and smoke and flames began to rise to the sky. Inga's eyes began to water as she realized that she would never go home again. Everyone and everything she loved had been taken away from her. She would probably never go back to school, never live with her mother, never see her brothers and sister. Even her cat, dog, and horse could not be found. She was by herself and the world looked dim and shadowed, the sunlight never *coming from the sky. Dark swirling clouds descended on her and soon she stood alone weeping for her loss.*

Inga wiped away the tears as she woke from her dream before the sun came up, unsure if meant anything. She dressed for work; she had to get the wood in the fireplaces lit before the family got up or she would again be punished. Soon the house was warmer and the rest of the family began to stir, so she could go to the kitchen for a breakfast of gruel and rye bread. She breathed in the smell of freshly baked bread and it reminded her of home a year ago. She blinked back the tears before the other servants could see her maudlin mood. Being weepy would get her nowhere, and she needed to adjust her attitude before the family laughed at her. She needed to show strength, not weakness, in the face of adversity. She would not let them see her suffer indignities because of her plight in life.

While sitting at the kitchen table, she heared a knock at the door. As the cook let someone in, Inga could see that it was Hanna and Henry for a surprise visit.

"We went to the front door but were told to come to the servant's entrance if we were to talk to you," announced Hanna petulantly. "Is that what you are here, a servant? That's not quite what *mor* was promised when she asked for them to take you."

"Well, that's what I am. A proper upstairs maid," said Inga. "I sew, mend, wash, iron and do all other duties as assigned. I'm so glad to see you though, don't bother about me. I'll survive until I can leave. What brings the two of you here?"

Hanna looked at Henry and then showed Inga a letter they had recently received from their brothers who were homesteading land near Calgary, Canada. With it was an ad from a newspaper for help wanted:

HELP WANTED:

Looking for Scandinavian workers who want to go to America. Willing to pay passage on a steamship if you will work for room, board, meals, and clothes for one year.

Looking for agriculture workers who can run a mule team for threshing wheat in North Dakota, Canada, and surrounding areas. Write to Box 17, Chicago Tribune.

Looking for Scandinavian worker who will assist a physician and learn trade of nursing. Must be a college graduate, speak English and Swedish. Will provide transportation to Chicago. Write to Box 28, Chicago Tribune.

The letter from Canada was an answer to Hanna's letter announcing the death of their father. The brothers, who were farming in Red Deer, Alberta, Canada, had a tiny home built on the property where they and their wives were living with their children. They sent the letter to encourage Hanna and maybe Henry to come to the United States and start a new life, since they no longer worked the farm or owned a home. Hanna wrote her *mor* and explained what the letter from her brothers said and asked her mother to send Henry to Stockholm. He took the train to Stockholm and they decided that Hanna would stop working in the factory and apply for the job as a nurse. Hanna wrote a reply for Henry, who would go also. Although he couldn't write, he was familiar with mules and threshing machines. Hanna had written letters to both employers and received replies that the jobs were available to them both as soon as they could arrive. Henry would also protect Hanna on the trip to Chicago, so they would get married that day and leave on the steamship out of Göteborg, Sweden, their tickets prepaid in their names.

"We're hoping that you and *mor* can come see us get married. We've got an appointment with the priest at 11a.m. today," said Hanna excitedly. "Do you think you will be able to come?"

Inga hurried to tell Aunt Mathilda the good news about Henry and Hanna and asked if she could walk with them to the church and watch them get married.

Aunt Mathilda's reply shocked Hanna. "No, you may not go to town. I don't care if she is your sister. You have work to do and it cannot wait."

Hanna looked at Inga with wide, unbelieving eyes and then said to their aunt, "You've got to be kidding me. She really can't go and see us married? She won't be long, two hours at the most!"

"No! Absolutely not! Inga will not leave the property. She has a job to do and she will stay and do it."

Inga's eyes grew cloudy and tears ran down her cheeks. "I guess I can't go, Hanna. If Aunt Mathilda turns me out for disobeying her, I'll have nowhere to go. But please write me and let me know about the service, the trip, the job, and what Henry is doing."

Hanna turned her back to her aunt and stepped away from her while mumbling under her breath. "I've never heard of such a thing. Any servant would be able to go for a special occasion. I may not see her again for years!"

Aunt Mathilda looked at Hanna with a smirk on her face. "Your family has lost everything and the only reason Inga is here is out of the goodness of my heart. She is lucky she hasn't been sent to the poor house for the sloppy work she does every day."

Inga cringed when the words left her aunt's mouth. She had tried so hard to do everything right, to show her aunt that she could work hard and never complain. Was it all in vain?

Hanna and Henry stepped out of the servant's door but did

not leave until the last barb was thrown. "I will write you every month, Inga, and send you a ticket for Chicago as soon as I can afford it, even if it takes me a year to earn the wages." And with that, they were gone.

Inga's feet dragged the rest of the day, her emotions on her sleeve. Just thinking about the fight with her aunt caused her eyes to mist over and her heart to break. She knew now that her aunt and uncle did not love her; in fact, they rejoiced in the fact that Inga was at their mercy and unable to escape. It was their gloating attitude that showed her that she would never be considered family and she would be a servant as long as she lived there.

That night Inga cried into her pillow, heaving great sighs for the life she was to lead. How did her life go from wonderful to horrible within a year? No one seemed to care about her, her friends never asked about her, her family was split into pieces, her cousins thought they were so much better than her and smirked at her on a daily basis. Inga could not see an end to her ordeal. She thought it would be better to be dead than to live the life she was living.

CHAPTER 12
June 1891

Day in and day out
The days seem the same for me
It does no good to cry or pout
Will love again come for me?
Will life come again to me?

Each day got easier for Inga as her small arms got stronger and her back did not hurt as much. But if the chores were not done in a timely fashion, her aunt would take the switch and hit her legs to speed her up. Her aunt seemed to relish hitting Inga, especially when she was in a bad mood, had argued with her husband, or was overly tired from yelling at the servants to do their jobs better. Several of the servants quit and moved on, but others had nowhere else to go and stayed, even with the punishments doled out by her aunt. Sometimes, Inga would hurry to do a chore and then her heart would speed up and she would have to slow down again. Sometimes she felt sick to her stomach and her head felt dizzy, but she continued to do the chores as best she could. Her clothes became too big as her body became muscular and svelte. Clothes that were loose on top suddenly became tight and her clothes no longer fit there. Her hips became rounder and her legs longer. Her courses became regular and Inga knew that she had matured into a woman. She wished that she could talk to her *mor* or Hanna about the changes that were happening, but she would never talk to her aunt or her cousins. They seemed to be angry with the way her body was changing. Boys talked to her on Sundays at church, and even the farm workers spoke to her while they ignored her cousins. Not only because of the class difference between rich and poor, because they all knew that Inga had once been rich, but because they now identified Inga with their class, as she was considered a servant, and a pretty one at that. Men in their thirties were looking to wed teenagers, as they were able to buy property and provide for a family. The men needed a young woman to provide them with children who could work their farms and have a boy to leave the farm to as an inheritance, while women did not inherit land even if it had been theirs by right. Women did not have a say in their family life. It was a man's world.

Even after more than a year, her uncle continued to come into her room at night and kiss her on her forehead and pat her blankets. But lately, he also curled Inga's hair around his fingers and said something nice to her, all the while looking at her with eyes that roamed her body. Inga was more nervous than ever. Her father never did that to any of the servants who worked for them at the farm. Why was Uncle Torvald being so nice? Inga had a suspicion that her uncle was not acting like he should toward a niece.

Inga fell asleep and dreamed of her life on the old farm. She missed her mother and sister and remembered the happy times.

Suddenly, her dream moved her to Vasakull and her life there. Her Uncle Torvald was in her bedroom, but this time, he did not stop to kiss her forehead; instead, he kissed her on the cheeks and neck. As Inga struggled against his advances and tried to pull the covers over her face, her uncle grabbed the blanket, put his hand under it, and rubbed his hand on her bosom. He persisted in rubbing his hands over her body and down to where her legs met. His hands were still over her clothes, but Inga could feel his hands trying to rub between her legs as he moaned and closed his eyes. Inga tried to scream, but her mouth was covered by his mouth as he tried to put his tongue into it. Struggling and kicking, Inga screamed, but the sound was blocked by his hand. His other hand threw back the covers and her uncle reached under her nightshirt, pressing his fingers into the cleft of her secret place, a private place where no one but her future husband was allowed to touch.

Suddenly, a bright light shown in her room and an angel appeared. Uncle Torvald disappeared and the angel took her hand and began singing the lullaby that Inga had heard the night her father died. Inga knew at that moment that something wrong was going to happen soon, and it was something to do with Uncle Torvald.

Inga woke with a start. Uncle Torvald was not the man her father had been; he had something planned and was building up to touching Inga in inappropriate places. What else would he do? Inga remembered her mother's warning about young men and the cover of night months before. Would a married man who was also her uncle do those things to her? Her dreams were always a warning, and she worried about doing nothing. Would her uncle continue to increase his behavior? Inga thought that perhaps she should talk to her mother the coming Sunday at church, her only time to see her.

The following Sunday, Inga looked for her mother at church but she didn't see her. She quickly went over to Fru Pehrsdotter's bench and sat down next to her.

"Fru Pehrsdotter, where is my *mor*?" asked Inga.

"Why, Inga, it's so nice to see you. I don't know, perhaps she is not feeling well today. What do you need?"

"I have to talk to her about my Uncle Torvald," whispered Inga. "I need to ask her if he is acting inappropriately."

"Why child, what has he done? Is he doing something you don't like at home?

"Yes," said Inga. "He is touching me at night and I am worried about what his intentions are."

"Oh my!" said Fru Pehrsdotter. "He should not be touching you at all. He should not be in your bedroom for any reason, as your Aunt Mathilda runs the house."

"What do you suggest I do or say to my uncle?

"I'm afraid he has gone too far already," said Fru Pehrsdotter. "You need to get out of that house as soon as you can. You must come to my house. Your grandmother has left some things for you, which she gave to me. She told me years ago that you would need to leave Sweden. I just didn't realize it would be so soon. You are only sixteen years old now, right?"

"Yes, but I am afraid to stay at my aunt's house."

"Come to my house this night and I will help you."

Inga thought about Hanna's last letter. She and Henry had married and sailed to America a month ago. They were staying with Swedish friends that had settled in Chicago, where other Swedes had gone. They were attending the Swedish Baptist church near the railroad stop and had joined the Vasa Society, a club that taught newly arrived Swedes how to speak English. Inga knew she could go to Chicago and be with her sister, who would find her a job. Jobs were plentiful in Chicago for upstairs maids and servants who knew how to sew, iron, and wash. Inga certainly had enough practice doing those jobs. That was where she would go. Hanna hadn't sent her any money, but perhaps Fru Pehrsdotter would loan her the money for the trip to America.

CHAPTER 13
June 1891

The night was dark
The moon was new
Nary a light in the forest shown through
Fairies cried
And even trolls wept
Sweden's child
Must find life anew.

Inga did her chores as if she would always be living in the house of her cousins, but silently through the day she packed a small bag of her clothes, shoes, and the small box containing the pink fairy, letters, and small piece of material. She included the diary that she had started when she was fourteen and living at her farm. She quickly put her bag under a bush near the road. When the full moon came out and the sun went down at 10 p.m., Inga would have plenty of time to walk away if all her chores were done. The house was only one mile from the church where last she saw her mother and so that evening, after an early dinner, she told her aunt that she would go to town for a few items now that her chores were finished for the day. Her aunt had no reason to believe that this would be the last day that Inga would be in her house and told her to hurry before the temperature dropped and the fireplaces would need to be stacked with wood.

Inga dressed in warm clothes and high boots, even though it was summer, then bade goodbye to her Aunt Mathilda and walked by the bush where her clothes were stashed, picked them up, and continued on her way to the little store, where she bought some food to eat on her journey. Inga had no idea what the weather would be like on her trip across the ocean and on the train to Chicago or when she would be eating again. Walking briskly, she passed the Lutheran church and said a quiet goodbye to her father at his grave site, then walked on to the *Folkhögskola* where she had attended *Midsommerfest* two years before. She had not been allowed to attend while living with her aunt. She turned down the path that would take her to Salsjö, the lake where she and her friends had swum many times as she was growing up. The entire time she walked, she tried not to think of trolls and wood nymphs that might catch her on her way, or the wolves or moose that might attack her. But if she had looked carefully, she would have seen the *hustomten* in the yards of the houses she passed, the trolls that hid behind the trees, and the small fairies who guided her through the forest to protect her from the wolves and moose. She thought only good thoughts and talked to the fairies who might help her on her journey this night. She asked the brownies in the woods to show her the way in the dark and they did. The trail to Salsjö was long and winding, at least two miles, and because it was summer the green leaves and sturdy tree roots crackled and made her trip as she walked. The ground was wet from the last rain and she would have to worry about mud. Finally, she saw the lake and stopped to rest for a few minutes, then decided to walk around it on the west side where a small trail stopped at the falls. It took her a while to make her way there and then down the slippery waterfall as the river continued on its way.

The brownies and the wood nymphs helped her even though they kept hidden from her sight. They whispered to her so quietly that she only heard the leaves in the trees.

Following past the waterfall and then beside a babbling brook on its way to the sea, she knew she must be at Vierydsån, the river that ran next to Fru Pehrsdotter's house and down to the harbor. Caught in vines and dense tree limbs, she sometimes had to crawl on her hands and knees to get through the forest of trees and sticker bushes. Between the mud and slippery leaves, she probably hiked another two miles, finally arriving at Fru Pehrsdotter's house at 11 p.m.. Straightening her hair and brushing the leaves and mud from her clothes, she knocked on the door of the home she loved to visit so well. Fru Pehrsdotter and her son were in the kitchen eating a late dinner when she arrived.

"Come in, child. Wash your hands and face and then have some food," Fru Pehrsdotter replied when Inga greeted her. Inga did what she was told and then sat down and ate some of the stew that was cooking on the old woodstove. Fru Pehrsdotter put a blanket on her shoulders to keep her from getting chilled from her walk in the woods and then motioned to her son to get the buggy out of the barn. As he left, Fru Pehrsdotter brought out a box of things Inga had never seen before. In it was old Swedish money, a purse to put it in, and a letter. "I've talked to your mother. She is not feeling well and won't be able to see you before you leave," said Fru Pehrsdotter. "She knew that this day was coming, though she didn't think it would come so fast, as I told you at church. Your grandmother had foretold your fleeing Sweden and had put these things away for you so you would have the means to get to America. Henry Thorsell and Hanna married last month and have gone to Chicago. They will meet you when you arrive. Here is the address to the Vasa House. Hanna has been looking for a job that you can do when you get there."

Inga was dumbfounded. When did all of these arrangements happen? Why didn't anyone tell her she'd be going to America?

Fru Pehrsdotter gave Inga a comforting look. "The family knew that this would all happen because your grandmother, God rest her soul, foretold it to your mother before she died. We have just been waiting for the time to come, and when Henry asked Hanna for her hand in marriage, we knew it was the beginning of the time when things would happen." Inga was amazed that this was all foretold twenty-five years ago. She knew then that her part would soon need to take place in the happenings.

Inga finished her meal and then looked in the box. The money was a large amount, enough to feed her and buy a ticket to America on a steamship and a train ticket to Chicago. She opened the letter and read her grandmother's words.

> *Inga, you will soon be on a journey to a new life. I see you traveling on a large ship to America and so I have left you money to go there. Do not be afraid. I will guard you on your trip and nothing will happen to you. But, you must be careful of people who would take advantage of a young girl traveling by herself. Keep your money around your waist and stay with other Swedish families so no one knows you are traveling alone. Be friendly, but very cautious of others who would do you harm. Don't worry; you will be back to Sweden many times in the future. And you will bring your own family with you.*
>
> *I love you, Grandma Ingaborg*

Inga looked at the small purse that was in the box. It was narrow and had a belt to go around her waist under her clothes. She put some bills into the purse and gave the rest to Herr Andresson to buy a ticket for Inga. She put the purse on and saw that it fit and was not too bulky. It would not be seen under her clothes and coat. Fru Pehrsdotter told Inga they would take her to the train station in Karlshamn because they worried that Aunt Mathilda would start looking for her at the Bräkne-Hoby train station since she had disappeared hours ago. Her mother would be at her sister's house so as not to arouse suspicion of her leaving.

Inga dried her clothes and swept the mud from her shoes and socks. She was so nervous that she shook, but Fru Pehrsdotter hugged her and talked to her all the way to the rail station, making her feel better about the journey she was about to take. Fru Pehrsdotter's son went to the station master and bought Inga a second-class train ticket to Göteborg, Sweden, where a boat would be waiting to take her to America. When Inga looked at the boat ticket she felt better; the boat was named *The America* and so she would sleep on the train and board the boat tomorrow afternoon. The trip to Göteborg would take five hours and she would arrive at the boat dock with six hours to spare. Then she would be on her way to a new life!

Inga bade Fru Pehrsdotter and her son goodbye as the train pulled up to the station at 1 a.m. As they kissed, Fru Pehrsdotter promised to give her mother a goodbye kiss for Inga. She found a seat next to a window so she could wave goodbye and send air kisses. She was so tired after hiking through the woods. She sat down, took a big breath, and felt her grandmother's hand in hers. Knowing that she would be watched over made her feel older than her sixteen years. She looked around and wondered how many others were going to America. She spied a family with lots of belongings with them and noted a boy of about eighteen years among the children seated with them. Inga smiled. Maybe the trip would not be so uneventful after all. She walked up to the family and asked the oldest girl, about her age, where they were traveling.

The entire family turned to Inga and said, "America." Inga quietly said that she was going to America also and the family immediately asked her to join them as they traveled. Not wanting to seem impolite, the Swedish family did not ask why Inga was traveling alone. She sat next to the girl and softly told them that she had a ticket on a boat leaving Göteborg, Sweden the following night and they told her that they would also be on that boat. They exchanged names and settled down to sleep while the train rocked them back and forth. Inga smiled to herself as she thought of her grandmother knowing the future so long ago. She was comforted by the knowledge that Hanna and Henry would be waiting for her in Chicago. Her only worry would be how she would get from New York to Chicago, but that would be another story for another time. For now, she would start a new page in her diary which read,

1891 June 13

I dag go I till Chicago. It is city jag no från Frau Anderson, who teach me English ven I er smal. Min sister Hanna vill hav en yob for me. Soon vill be min forst dag as American. I vill spak English so no man nos jag komma från Sweden. I vill hav nu nam so no man fran Sweden vill no me. I vill go till skol and I vill get rich and go till Sweden to get min mor...

If Inga had looked out the window of the train, she might have seen elves, fairies, brownies, *hustomten*, and even the trolls bidding her goodbye with tears in their eyes.

Thank you for reading Inga's story. The next book contains her adventure on the ship, *The America*. Be sure to look for it soon.

PRONUNCIATION GUIDE

Word	Pronounce It Like:	Means
Akuavit	ah-qua-veet	Swedish vodka
bergakungen	ber- ga-koon-yen	hall of the mountain king
blåkulla,	blo-kool-a	a place where witches live
Bräkne-Hoby	brak-ne Hoo-bee	town in southern Sweden
de Kloka	dee klock-a	wise one, witch
djävular	ya-vu-lar	devils
Döden är vår Herres sopkvast	do-den-ar-vor-Her-res -sop-kvast	Death is our Lord's broom
dra ät häklefjäl	dra-at-ha-lef-yol	I'll see you in Hell
far	far	father
folkhögskola	folk-hog-sko-la	trade school after grammar school
första	for-sta	first
från	fran	from
fru	fru	Mrs.
gå igen	go i-yen	reappear
gast, spoke	gast, spok	ghosts
Göteborg, (Gothenburg)	Yo-ti-bor-ie	city in southern Sweden
gröt	groot	oat cereal
hej	hay	hello
herr	har	Mr.
Hjälmseryd	yal-mes-rude	farm name
hustomten, 'tomte	hoos-tom-ten	house brownie
I dag, dag	ee-dag, dag	today, day
Jag behover inte vakna sig upp.	yag be-hover in-te vak-na say oop	I do not want to wake up

Word	Pronounce It Like:	Means
Jansson's Temptation	Yan-sens temp-tation	potatoes and fish
Jul	Yul	Christmas
julfest	Yul-fest	Christmas party
komma	Koom-ma	come
Lagom ä bäst	la-goom a baast	right is best
långhus	long-hus	long house
Midsommerfest	mid-summer-fest	June 21st festival
min	min	my
mor, mor mor	more	mother, mother's mother (grandmother)
öre	or-ee	penny
Otack ä värdens ïon	o-tak a var-dems ee-on	The world's reward is ingratitude
Överhogdal	ov-er-hog-dal	tapestry
rosemaling	rose-mal-ing	painting technique
Salsjö	sal-sho	lake's name
Schottische	shot-tish	folk dance
Skogrä,	skoo-gra	wood nymphs
skola	skool-la	school
skymning	shym-ning	twilight
Små grytor ha också öron	smo gree-to ha ok-so or-en	Small pitchers have big ears
Tack	tak	thank you
tala	tal-a	speak
till	til	to
trollbarn	troll-barn	troll children
Vasakull	vas-a-kul	farm name
Vierydfjorden	vi-er-id-fee-yor-den	harbor at end of river
Vierydsån	vi-er-id-son	the river's name
Ystmote	u-st-mot	cheese making

ABOUT THE AUTHOR

Barbara is considered a renaissance woman, as she not only writes and paints, but also plays multiple instruments, sings, and has a Master's Degree in International Affairs. She spent three months in Sweden researching her great grandmother's life and learning the language, and has studied Russian also. She has taught college several years and worked for many years as a high school teacher in Northern California.